THE BIGGER
THEY COME

ERLE STANLEY GARDNER (1889-1970) was the best-selling American author of the 20th century, mainly due to the enormous success of his Perry Mason series, which numbered more than 80 novels and inspired a half-dozen motion pictures, radio programs, and a long-running television series that starred Raymond Burr. Having begun his career as a pulp writer, Gardner brought a hard-boiled style and sensibility to the early Mason books and to his series starring Bertha Cool and Donal Lam. For over a quarter of a century he wrote more than a million words a year under his own name and numerous pseudonyms, the most famous being A.A. Fair.

OTTO PENZLER, the creator of American Mystery Classics, is also the founder of the Mysterious Press (1975), a literary crime imprint; MysteriousPress.com (2011), an electronic-book publishing company; Penzler Publishers (2018); and New York City's Mysterious Bookshop (1979). He has won a Raven, the Ellery Queen Award, two Edgars (for the *Encyclopedia of Mystery and Detection*, 1977, and *The Lineup*, 2010), and lifetime achievement awards from NoirCon and *The Strand Magazine*. He has edited more than 70 anthologies and written extensively about mystery fiction.

THE BIGGER
THEY COME

ERLE STANLEY GARDNER

writing as A. A. Fair

Introduction by
OTTO
PENZLER

AMERICAN
MYSTERY
CLASSICS

Penzler Publishers
New York

Published in 2022 by Penzler Publishers
58 Warren Street, New York, NY 10007
penzlerpublishers.com

Distributed by W. W. Norton

Cover image: Andy Ross
Cover design: Mauricio Diaz

Paperback ISBN 978-1-61316-356-6
Hardcover ISBN 978-1-61316-357-3

Library of Congress Control Number: 2022906674

Printed in the United States of America

9 8 7 6 5 4 3 2 1

INTRODUCTION

When readers think about Erle Stanley Gardner, they mostly conjure Perry Mason, partly for the eighty-six novels in which the trial lawyer was the primary character, but also for the long-running television series that starred Raymond Burr and is still a late-night staple in re-runs.

But Gardner also wrote thirty novels under the A.A. Fair pseudonym, all about the private detectives Bertha Cool and Donald Lam. *The Bigger They Come* (titled *Lam to the Slaughter* in the U.K.), the first novel in the series, was published in 1939, but Gardner's authorship was not revealed until the end of World War II. For most authors, thirty books would be a full career but for Gardner it was fewer than a quarter of the 130 novels he produced.

Many readers prefer the novels about this unlikely detective duo to his more iconic defense lawyer because the characterization is sharper than in the Mason and other novels and they have the one element noticeably lacking in much of Gardner's other works—humor.

Bertha Cool is the senior member of the team. A large, gray-haired woman in her sixties, she founded the private investigation agency in 1936 when her husband Henry Cool died. Her twinkling eyes give her a grandmotherly appearance that is belied by her tough-mindedness and equally tough language. Her battles with weight are an ongoing challenge, as she has weighed as much as 275 pounds. She prefers to wear loose, unconfining garments and has been described by her partner as looking like "a cylinder of current jelly on a plate" when she walks.

Donald Lam is a disbarred lawyer who has had many brushes with the police. In *The Bigger They Come* he is hungry, desperately in need of a job, and he manages to convince Mrs. Cool that, despite his diminutive appearance—he is five feet, six inches, tall and weighs 125 pounds—he is man enough to be a detective. He tries to prove it by never backing down from a fight but usually gets beat up. Though small, he is considered very attractive by most women, though Elsie Brand, the firm's pretty and shy secretary, proves elusive in spite of Lam's relentless pursuit.

After being hired by Mrs. Cool, Lam's first assignment is simply to serve a subpoena but he is unable to locate the man. In fact, no one seems able to find him.

As it happens, the book was based on a real-world quirk in the law that Gardner, a lawyer, discovered and, as a crusader for much of his life, wove into the plot. He learned that there are certain conditions in Arizona that made it possible to commit murder with impunity as long as the murderer never left the state. Although a work of fiction, when it was published lawmakers were made aware of this loophole in the law and closed it.

There were numerous elements in the Cool-Lam series that returned on a regular basis. References to Mrs. Cool's weight are common (with various books listing it between 160 and 275 pounds), as are numerous mentions of her avaricious greed and her foul mouth, though the most common epithet quoted is the mild, if bizarre, "fry me for an oyster."

Most books remind readers of Lam's quick wit and profound knowledge of the law. Although he often is referred to as disbarred, he claims he wasn't ever officially disbarred but that he merely talked to much. When Bertha asks him what he talked too much about, he is both embarrassed and feisty when he acknowledges that he told someone how he could commit a murder and get away with it. (Although the methods were different, other lawyers in fiction—and, let's be honest, probably in real life—explained to clients that murder was the solution to their problems, notably Melville Davisson Post's Randolph Mason and Lawrence Block's Ehrengraf.)

Gardner's style changed quite a bit over the years. He started his career as a writer for the pulp magazines that flourished in the 1920s and 1930s. Authors were famously paid a penny a word by most of the pulps, but the top writers in the top magazines managed to get all the way up to three cents a word. This munificent fee was reserved for the best of the best of their time, some of whom remain popular and successful to the present day (Dashiell Hammett, Raymond Chandler, Cornell Woolrich), some of whom only are remembered and read by the modest coterie that avidly reads and collects pulp fiction (Carroll John Daly, Arthur Leo Zagat, Arthur J. Burks). One who earned the big bucks regularly, especially when he wrote for *Black Mask*, the greatest of the pulps, was Erle Stanley Gardner.

Gardner had learned and honed his craft in the pulps, so it is not surprising that the earliest Perry Mason novels were hardboiled, tough-guy books, with Mason as a fearless, two-fisted battler, rather than the calm, self-possessed figure that most readers remember today. Reading the first Mason novels, *The Case of the Velvet Claws*, published in 1933, and *The Case of the Careless Kitten*, published twenty years later, it is difficult to remember that they were written by the same author. Both styles, by the way, were first-rate, just different.

Gardner was born in Malden, Massachusetts, in 1889. Because his father was a mining engineer, he traveled often as a child. As a teenager, he participated in professional boxing as well as promoting unlicensed matches, placing himself at risk of criminal prosecution, which gave him an interest in the law. He took a job as a typist at a California law firm and after reading law for fifty hours a week for three years, he was admitted to the California bar. He practiced in Oxnard from 1911 to 1918, gaining a reputation as a champion of the underdog through his defense of poor Mexican and Chinese clients.

He left to become a tire salesman in order to earn more money but he missed the courtroom and joined another law firm in 1921. It is then that he started to write fiction, hoping that he could augment his modest income. He worked a full day at court, followed that with several hours of research in the law library, then went home to write fiction into the small hours, setting a goal of at least 4,000 words a day. He sold two stories in 1921, none in 1922, and only one in 1923, but it was to the prestigious *Black Mask*. The following year, thirteen of his stories saw print, five of them in *Black Mask*. Over the next decade he wrote nearly fifteen million words and sold hundreds of stories, many pseudonymously so that he could have multiple stories in a single magazine, each under a different name.

His output was prodigious. He wrote 1,200,000 words annually during most of the 1920s and 1930s. That is a novel a month, plus a stack of short stories, for a fifteen-year stretch. In 1932, his most productive year, he wrote an unimaginable 2,400,000 words—the equivalent of a full-length novel every other week.

In 1932, he finally took a vacation, an extended trip to China, since he had become so financially successful. That is also the year in which he began to submit his first novel, *The Case of the Velvet Claws*. It was rejected by several publishers before William Morrow took it, and Gardner published every mystery with that house for the rest of his life. Thayer Hobson, then the president of Morrow, suggested that the protagonist of that book, Perry Mason, should become a series character and Gardner agreed.

The Mason novels became an immediate success so Gardner resigned from his law practice to devote full time to writing. Eager to have privacy, he acquired parcels of land in the Southwest and eventually settled into the "Gardner Fiction Factory" on a thousand-acre ranch in Temecula, California. The ranch had a dozen guest cottages and trailers to house his support staff of twenty employees, all of whom are reported to have called him "Uncle Erle." Among them were six secretaries, all working full time, transcribing his dictated novels, non-fiction books and articles, and correspondence.

He was intensely interested in prison conditions and was a strong advocate of reform. In 1948, he formed the Court of Last Resort, a private organization dedicated to helping those believed to have been unfairly incarcerated. The group succeeded in freeing many unjustly convicted men and Gardner wrote a book, *The Court of Last Resort*, describing the group's work; it won an Edgar for the best fact crime book of the year.

In the 1960s, Gardner became alarmed at some changes in American literature. He told the *New York Times*, "I have always aimed my fiction at the masses who constitute the solid backbone of America, I have tried to keep faith with the American family. In a day when the prevailing mystery story trends are towards sex, sadism, and seduction, I try to base my stories on speed, situation, and suspense."

While Gardner wrote prolifically about a wide variety of characters under many pseudonyms, most notably the thirty novels about Cool and Lam, all his books give evidence of clearly identifiable characteristics. There is a minimum of description and a maximum of dialogue, and Gardner's heroes are not averse to breaking the exact letter of the law in order to secure what they consider to be justice. They share contempt for pomposity. Villains or deserving victims are often self-important, wealthy individuals who can usually be identified because Gardner has given them two last names (such as Harrington Faulkner).

Whether the books feature Perry Mason, D.A. Doug Selby, Bertha Cool and Donald Lam, or non-series characters, Erle Stanley Gardner's writing always entertains. You don't sell more than 300,000,000 books by failing to deliver.

—OTTO PENZLER

CHAPTER ONE

PUSHING MY way into the office, I stood just inside the door, my hat in my hand.

There were six men ahead of me. The ad had said between the ages of twenty-five and thirty. If appearances were any indication, some of them were optimistic liars. For the most part, we were a seedy-looking outfit.

A straw-haired secretary behind a typewriting desk banged away at a typewriter. She looked up at me. Her face was as cold as a clean bedsheet.

"What do you want?" she asked.

"I want to see Mr. Cool."

"What about?"

I moved my head in a comprehensive gesture to include the half-dozen men who were looking up at me in casually hostile appraisal. "I'm answering the ad."

"I thought so. Sit down," she said.

"There seems," I observed, "to be no chair available."

"There will be in a minute. You may stand and wait, or come back."

"I'll stand."

She turned back to her typewriter. A buzzer sounded. She

picked up a telephone, listened a moment, said, "Very well," and looked expectantly at the door which said "B. L. Cool, Private." The door opened. A man, who looked as though he was trying to get to the open air in a hurry, streaked through the office. The blonde said, "You may go in, Mr. Smith."

A young chap with stooped shoulders and slim waist got to his feet, jerked down his vest, adjusted his tie, pinned a smirk on his face, opened the door to the private office, and went in.

The blonde said to me, "What's your name?"

"Donald Lam."

"L-a-m-b?" she asked.

"L-a-m," I said.

She jotted it down, and then, with her eyes on me, started making shorthand notes under the name. I could see she was cataloguing my personal appearance.

"That all?" I asked when she'd covered me from head to foot with her eyes and finished making pothooks with her fingers.

"Yes. Sit down in that chair and wait."

I sat and waited. Smith didn't last long. He was out in less than two minutes. The second man made the round trip so fast it looked as though he'd come out on the bounce. The third man lasted ten minutes and came out looking dazed. The door of the outer office opened. Three more applicants came in. The blonde took their names, sized them up and made notes. After they were seated, she picked up the telephone and said laconically, "Four more," listened for a moment, and hung up.

When the next man came out, the blonde went in. She was in there about five minutes. When she came out, she gave me the nod: "You may go in next, Mr. Lam," she said.

The men who were ahead of me frowned at her and then at me. They didn't say anything.

Apparently she didn't mind their frowns any more than I did.

I opened the door, entered a huge room with several filing cabinets, two comfortable chairs, a table, and a big desk.

I put on my best smile, said, "Mr. Cool, I—" and then stopped, because the person seated behind the desk wasn't Mister.

She was somewhere in the sixties, with gray hair, twinkling gray eyes, and a benign, grandmotherly expression on her face. She must have weighed over two hundred. She said, "Sit down, Mr. Lam—no, not in that chair. Come over here where I can look at you. There, that's better. Now, for Christ's sake, don't lie to me."

She swung around in her swivel chair and looked me over. I might have been her favorite grandson coming in for a cookie. "Where do you live?" she asked.

"I haven't any permanent address," I said. "Right at present I'm in a rooming house on West Pico."

"What's your training?"

"Nothing," I told her, "that does me any good. I had an education that was supposed to fit me for the appreciation of art, literature, and life. It didn't have anything to do with making money. I find I can't appreciate art, literature, or life without money."

"How old are you?"

"Twenty-eight."

"Parents living?"

"No."

"You're not married?"

"No."

She said, "You're just a little shrimp. I don't s'pose you weigh over a hundred and twenty, do you?"

"A hundred and twenty-seven."

"Can you fight?"

"No—I do sometimes, but I get licked."

"This is a *man's* job."

"And I'm a man," I retorted hotly.

"But you're too small. People would push you around."

"When I was in college," I said, "some of the boys used to try it. They gave it up after a while. I don't like to be pushed around. There are lots of ways of fighting. I have my way, and I'm good at it."

"Did you read the ad carefully?"

"I think I did."

"Did you consider yourself qualified?"

"I have no ties on earth," I said. "I think I'm fairly courageous. I'm active, and, I hope, intelligent. If I'm not, somebody wasted a lot of money giving me an education."

"Who?"

"My father."

"When did he die?"

"Two years ago."

"What have you been doing since then?"

"Odd jobs."

Her face didn't change expression. She smiled at me benignly and said, "You're a God-awful liar."

I pushed back my chair.

"Being a woman," I said, "you can call me that. Being a man, I don't have to take it."

I started for the door.

"Wait a minute," she said. "I think you stand a chance of getting the job."

"I don't want it."

"Don't be a sap. Turn around here and look at me. You *were* lying, weren't you?"

What the hell! The job was gone anyway. I swung around and faced her. "Yes," I said, "I was. It's a habit I have. Oddly enough, however, I prefer to have my prevarications called to my attention in a more tactful manner."

"Ever been in jail?"

"No."

"Come back here and sit down."

That's what pounding the pavement does for your morale. I went back and sat down. I had exactly ten cents in my pocket. I hadn't eaten since yesterday noon. The employment agencies either couldn't or wouldn't do a thing for me. I'd finally resorted to answering the ads that looked just a little fishy on their face. That's the last step.

"Now tell me the truth," she said.

"I'm twenty-nine," I told her. "My parents are dead. I've had a college education. I'm reasonably intelligent. I'm willing to do almost anything. I need the money. If you give me the job, I'll try and be loyal."

"Is that all?" she asked.

"That's all."

"What's your name?"

I smiled.

"Then I take it Lam isn't your real name?"

I said, "I've told you the truth. Now, I can keep on talking if you want—I'm rather good at that."

"I fancy you are," she said. "Now tell me, what did you really study in college?"

"What difference does that make?"

"I don't know, I'm sure," she said. "But it was the way you

answered questions about your college education that made me realize you were lying. You never went to college, now, did you?"

"Yes."

"You didn't graduate?"

"Yes, I did."

"You weren't expelled?"

"No."

She pursed her lips. "Do you know anything about anatomy?"

"No, not much."

"What did you study in college?"

"Want me to improvise?" I asked.

"No," she said. "Not now—yes, I do, too. This job needs a liar. It also needs a convincing talker. I didn't like your first lie. It wasn't convincing."

"I'm telling you the truth, now," I pointed out.

"Quit it, then. Lie to me for a while."

"What about?"

"Anything," she said, "only make it sound convincing. Build it up. Embroider it. What did you study in college?"

"The love life of microbes," I said. "So far scientists have only considered the propagation of microbes in terms of guinea pigs. No one has ever considered it from the standpoint of the microbe. Now, when I refer to the love life of a microbe, you are doubtless inclined to interpret it in terms of your own—"

"I haven't any," she interrupted.

"—outlook on life," I went on smoothly without paying any attention to her interruption. "Now, given an even temperature, a reasonable amount of nourishing food, microbes become exceedingly ardent. In fact, the—"

She held up her hand palm outward as though she were pushing the words back in my mouth. "That's enough of that

God damn tripe," she said. "It's glib but it isn't good lying because nobody cares. Tell me the truth. *Do* you know one single damn thing about microbes?"

"No," I told her.

Her eyes glittered. "How did you stop them from pushing you around when you were in college?"

"I'd prefer not to go into that—if you want the truth."

"I want the truth, and I want the information."

"I use my head. I *have* been called mean," I said. "Everyone has to protect himself in life. When he's weak somewhere, nature makes him strong elsewhere. I figure things out. I always have. If a man starts pushing me around, I find a way to make him stop, and before I'm through he's sorry he ever started pushing. I don't mind hitting below the belt if I have to. I guess I even get a kick out of it. That's because of the way I'm made. A little runt is apt to be mean.

"Now if you're through amusing yourself at my expense, I'll be going. I hate being laughed at. Some day you'll find it's been rather expensive amusement. I'll work out a scheme and get even with *you*."

She sighed, not the wheezy sigh of a fatigued fat woman, but a sigh that marked a load off her mind. She picked up the telephone on her desk, and said, "Elsie, Donald Lam gets the job. Clear that riffraff out of the office. Put a sign on the door that the position has been filled. There have been enough bums in the office for one day."

She slammed the receiver back on its hook, opened a drawer, took out some papers and started reading. After a few moments, I heard the scrape of chairs and muffled sounds from the outer office as the waiting applicants filed out.

I sat still, speechless with surprise, waiting.

"Got any money?" the woman asked abruptly.

"Yes," I said, and then added after a moment, "some."

"How much?"

"Enough to last me," I told her, "for a while."

She looked at me over the tops of her bifocal glasses, and said, "Amateurish lying again. It's worse than the microbes. That shirt's in bad shape. You can get one for eighty-five cents. Throw that necktie away. You can get a good one for twenty-five or thirty-five cents. Get your shoes shined. Get a haircut. I suppose your socks are full of holes. Are you hungry?"

"I'm all right," I said.

"For God's sake, don't pull that line with me. My God, look at yourself in the mirror. Your complexion is like a fish's belly. Your cheeks are hollow, and there are dark spots under your eyes. I'll bet you haven't eaten for a week. Go get yourself a good breakfast. We'll figure twenty cents for that, and you've got to do something about a suit, but you can't do that today. You're working for me now, and I don't want you to get the idea you can go shopping on my time. You can get a suit of clothes after five o'clock tonight. I'll give you an advance on salary, and God help you if you double-cross me on it. Here, here's twenty dollars."

I took the money.

"All right," she said; "be back here by eleven. Get started."

As I reached the door, she raised her voice. "Now listen, Donald, don't you go blowing that money. Twenty-five cents is absolutely tops on breakfast."

CHAPTER TWO

THE SECRETARY was banging away on the typewriter when I opened the door of the office which said "B. L. COOL—*Confidential Investigations.*"

"Hello," I said.

She nodded.

"Is—er—what is she, Mrs. or Miss?"

"Mrs."

"Is she in?"

"No."

"What," I asked, "do I call *you* besides 'say'?"

"Miss Brand."

I said, "I'm pleased to meet you, Miss Brand. I'm Donald Lam. Mrs. Cool hired me to fill the position mentioned in the ad."

She went on typing.

"Since I'm going to work here," I went on, "I expect we'll be seeing quite a bit of each other. You don't like me, and I don't think I'm going to like you. You can let it go at that if you want to."

She stopped typing to turn over a page on her shorthand

book. She looked up at me and said, "Oh, all right," and dropped her fingers back to the keyboard.

I walked over and sat down.

"Anything for me to do except wait?" I asked after a few minutes.

She shook her head.

"Mrs. Cool told me to be back here by ten."

"You're here," she said, and went on clacking away at the typewriter.

I took a package of cigarettes from my pocket. I'd been without smokes for a week, not because I wanted to, but because I had to.

The door of the outer office opened. Mrs. Cool came barging into the room with a trim-looking chestnut-haired trick a step behind her.

I sized up my new boss as she walked across the office, and revised my first estimate of her weight by adding twenty pounds. She evidently didn't believe in confining herself to tight clothes. She wiggled and jiggled around inside her loose apparel like a cylinder of currant jelly on a plate. But she wasn't wheezy, and she didn't waddle. She walked with a smooth, easy rhythm. It wasn't a stride. You weren't conscious of her legs at all. She flowed past like a river.

I looked at the girl behind her, and the girl looked at me.

She was trim-ankled, slender, and seemed to have her body and mind on frightened tip-toes. I had the impression that if I'd yell "*Boo!*" at the top of my voice, she'd be out of the office in two bounds. She had deep brown eyes, suntanned skin— or powder—and clothes which were cut to show her figure and did. It was a figure worth showing.

Elsie Brand kept right on typing.

Mrs. Cool held open the door of her private office. "Go right on in, Miss Hunter," she said, and then, looking at me, went on in the same tone of voice, almost as part of the same sentence, "I'm going to want you in five minutes. Wait."

The door closed.

I made myself as comfortable as possible and waited.

After a while, the telephone on Elsie Brand's desk buzzed. She stopped typing, picked up the receiver, said, "Very well," dropped the receiver back into place, and nodded at me. "Go on in," she said. She was back pounding the keys of the typewriter before I'd got out of the chair.

I opened the door to the private office. Mrs. Cool was overflowing the big swivel chair as she sat hunched up against the desk, her elbows leaning on it. As I opened the door, she was saying, "—no, dearie, I don't give a damn now how much you lie. We find out the truth sooner or later anyway; and the longer it takes to find out the truth, the more time we get paid for— this is Donald Lam. Mr. Lam, Miss Hunter. Mr. Lam hasn't been with me long, but he has the qualifications. He'll work on your case. I'll supervise what he does."

I bowed to the girl. She smiled at me in a preoccupied way. She seemed to be hesitating over some important decision.

Mrs. Cool, perfectly at ease, continued to hold down the desk with her elbows. She had that motionless immobility which characterizes the very fat. Thin people are constantly making jerky motions to alleviate the nervous pressure which possesses them. Mrs. Cool didn't have a fidget in her system. When she sat down, she was placed. She had the majesty of a snow-capped mountain, the assurance of a steam roller.

"Sit down, Donald," she said.

I sat down, taking a professional interest in Miss Hunter's profile—long, straight nose, fine chin, smooth, delicately shaped forehead, framed by glossy waves of chestnut hair. Her mind was occupied with some thought which drained all of her attention away from her present surroundings.

Mrs. Cool said to me, "You read the newspapers, Donald?"

I nodded.

"You've read about Morgan Birks?"

"A little," I said, fascinated by Miss Hunter's abstraction. "Wasn't he the one who was indicted by the grand jury in that slot-machine scandal?"

"There wasn't any scandal about it," Mrs. Cool said in a matter-of-fact tone of voice. "They had a lot of illegal slot-machines placed where they'd do the most good and naturally there was a pay-off to the police department. Morgan did the paying. The grand jury didn't indict him. They can't get enough evidence to indict him. They subpoenaed him as a witness. He didn't show up. They're trying to find him. There's some sort of a warrant out for him. That's all. If they get him, they can do something about the police department. If they don't get him, they can't. Why the hell anybody wants to call it a scandal is more than I know. It's just ordinary, routine business."

"I was quoting the newspapers," I said.

"Don't do it, Donald. It's a bad habit."

"What about Morgan Birks?" I asked, noticing that Miss Hunter was still very much occupied with her own thoughts.

"Morgan Birks has a wife," Mrs. Cool said. "Her name is—is—" She said to Miss Hunter, "Let's have those papers, dearie," and had to ask the second time before Miss Hunter suddenly snapped to attention, opened her purse, took out some folded, legal-looking documents, and handed them across the desk. Mrs. Cool picked up the papers and calmly resumed her conversation at the point where she'd interrupted herself, "—Sandra Birks. Sandra Birks wants a divorce. She's been figuring on it for some time. Morgan played into her hands by getting mixed up in this grand jury business. It's a swell time to get a divorce except for one thing. She can't find him to serve the papers."

"He's classed as a fugitive from justice?" I asked.

"I don't know how much justice there is about it," she said, "but he's sure as hell a fugitive from something. He can't be found."

"What am I to do?" I asked.

"Find him," she said, and slid the papers across the desk to me.

I picked up the papers. There was an original summons in the case *Birks versus Birks,* and a copy of the summons to which was attached a copy of the plaintiff's complaint.

Mrs. Cool said, "You don't have to be an officer to serve a summons. Any citizen of the United States over the age of twenty-one years and not a party to the action can make the service. Find Birks, serve him. When you make the service, you hand him the copy of the summons and the complaint. You show him the original summons, then you come back here and make an affidavit."

"How do I go about finding him?" I asked.

Miss Hunter said suddenly, "I think I can help you."

"And when I've found him," I asked Mrs. Cool, "will he resent—?"

Miss Hunter interrupted quickly, "And I know he will. That's the thing I'm afraid of. Mr. Lam might get hurt. Morgan is—"

Mrs. Cool interposed a calm, matter-of-fact, "My God, Donald, that's your headache. What the hell do you want us to do? Go along with you so you can hide behind our petticoats when you poke the summons out at him?"

I made up my mind she was going to fire me sooner or later anyhow. It might as well be now. "I was asking," I said, "for information."

"Well, you got your information."

"I don't think I did," I told her, "and in case you're interested, I don't like the way it was given."

She didn't even turn her eyes toward me. "I'm not interested," she said, and lifted the lid from the cigarette case on her desk. "Want to smoke, Miss Hunter—what the hell's your first name, dearie? I don't go much for last names."

"Alma."

"Want to smoke, Alma?"

"No, thank you. Not right now."

Mrs. Cool picked up a match, scraped it explosively against the underside of the desk, held it to the cigarette, and said, "As I was saying, Donald, you'll find Birks and serve the summons on him. Alma's going to help you find him—oh yes, you'll want to know where Alma fits into the picture. She's a friend of the wife—or is it a relative, dearie?"

"No, just a friend," Alma Hunter said. "Sandra and I roomed together before she got married."

"How long ago was that?" Mrs. Cool asked.

"Two years."

"Where are you living now?"

"With Sandra. She has an apartment with two bedrooms. I'm staying with her, and her brother is coming out from the East—you see, Morgan just packed up and left, and—"

"You know Morgan, of course?" Mrs. Cool interrupted.

"No," Alma Hunter said a little too quickly. "I never approved of—well, of the idea. Through Sandra, I knew things about him—I think I'd prefer not to go into that if you don't mind."

"I don't mind," Mrs. Cool said. "If you're referring to facts which don't enter into the case, they're none of my damn business. If they do, I'd a lot rather find them out for myself, at so many dollars a day, than have you tell me about them. Write your own ticket, dearie."

I saw the glint of a smile in Alma Hunter's eyes.

"And don't mind me when I cuss," Mrs. Cool went on, "because I like profanity, loose clothes, and loose talk. I want to be comfortable. Nature intended me to be fat. I put in ten years eating salads, drinking skimmed milk, and toying with dry toast. I wore girdles that pinched my waist, form-building brassières, and spent half of my time standing on bathroom scales.

"And what the hell did I do it for? Just to get a husband!"

"You got one?" Alma Hunter asked, her eyes showing her interest.

"Yes."

Miss Hunter was discreetly silent. Mrs. Cool resented the implications of her silence. "It wasn't that way at all," she said. "But hell, this isn't the time for a dissertation on my private life."

"I'm so sorry," Miss Hunter said. "Really, Mrs. Cool I didn't mean to be prying. I was just terribly interested. I'm—well, I have problems of my own—I don't like to hear people talk cynically about marriage. I think that when a woman really works to make a success of marriage, she can make the home so attractive that her husband wants to be there all the time. After two—"

"And why the hell should a woman do that for any man?" Bertha Cool interrupted in a calm, level voice. "My God, men don't own the world."

"But it's a woman's place in life," Alma Hunter said. "It's part of the biological structure."

Bertha Cool looked over the tops of her glasses. "If you want to talk biological urges," she said, "talk with Donald. He knows all about the courtship of microbes."

"Men aren't microbes," Alma Hunter said.

Bertha Cool sighed, and the sigh rippled the loose flesh of her stomach and breasts into jelly-like action. "Now listen," she said, "my marriage is the one thing on earth I am touchy about. Some day Donald's going to hear from someone all about what a bitch I was and how I treated my husband. I'll probably tell him the whole story myself, but I'll be damned careful I do it after office hours—unless I do it on *your* time, dearie—but for God's sake don't get married with the idea of putting a man upon a pedestal and yourself down on your hands and knees, scraping cobwebs out of the corner. You keep on doing that, and some day a cute little trick will look up at your husband with big blue eyes, and you'll find that you're in the place you made for yourself, just a damn floor scraper with rough hands, sharp features, and calloused knees—I know what you're thinking, that your husband won't be like that, but all husbands are like that."

"But, Mrs. Cool—"

"All right, if you want to go into details, listen to what happened in my case. And you listen, too, Donald. It'll do you good."

"It doesn't make any difference to me," I said. "For all I care, you could have—"

"Shut up," she said. "I'm your boss. Don't interrupt me when I'm talking." She turned back to Alma Hunter and said, "You get that idea about husbands out of your head, or you'll be unhappy as long as you live. My husband was an average specimen—as husbands go, and that's not very far. I kept on my diet until the glamour wore off, then I commenced to look across the breakfast table at him and wonder what the hell I was getting in return for what I was giving. He could eat peaches and cream, a big bowl of oatmeal swimming in butter, ham and eggs, coffee with thick cream, with two teaspoonfuls of sugar, and never put on a pound. He ate breakfasts like that right in front of my face. I sat across the table from him with my stomach begging me on its bended knees for just one spoonful of oatmeal, and I broke off dry toast and nibbled at little pieces of it so one piece would last through my husband's breakfast.

"And then the day came when he told me he had to be away in Chicago on business. I was suspicious and hired a detective to shadow him. He took his secretary and went down to Atlantic City. I got the report by telephone on Monday morning just as we were sitting down to breakfast."

Alma Hunter's eyes were sparkling.

"You divorced him?" she asked.

"Divorce, hell!" Mrs Cool said. "Why should I divorce the worm? He was my meal ticket. I just said, 'God damn you, Henry Cool, if you're going to take that peroxided hussy down to Atlantic City over weekends and make me like it, I'm going to eat what I please and make you like it.' So I dished myself out a big bowl of oatmeal, put so much butter on it that it was simply swimming, poured on thick whipping cream, puts lots of sugar on top of that, and scraped the bowl clean before my husband had got up his nerve enough to try and lie to me."

"Then what?" Alma asked.

"Oh," she said airily, "he kept on lying, and I kept on eating. After that, we worked out a pretty good basis of companionship. He kept on supporting me, and I kept on eating. He kept on playing around with the peroxide secretary until she tried to blackmail him. Well, of course I couldn't stand for that, so I went down and gave the little bitch a piece of my mind, and sent her on her way with her ears pinned back. And then *I* picked him a secretary."

"One who offered no possible temptation, I suppose," Alma Hunter said, with a smile.

"Not at all," Mrs. Cool said. "I was getting pretty fat by that time, and decided Henry should have a break. I picked him a good-looking little trick that I'd known for three years. I had enough on her so she didn't dare to blackmail him. And I swear to you, dearie, I don't know to this day whether Henry ever made her or not—but of course he did. I know that she liked to play around, and Henry just couldn't keep his hands off a woman. But she was a damn good secretary; and Henry seemed happy; and I ate anything I wanted. It was a wonderful arrangement—until Henry died."

She blinked her eyes, and I couldn't be certain whether it was a gesture or if there were tears glinting in the corners. Abruptly she was back to business. "You want a summons served. I'll serve it. Now what the hell more is there to talk about?"

"Nothing," Alma Hunter said, "except the matter of fees."

"This Sandra Birks has money?"

"She's not wealthy but she has—"

"Make me a check for a hundred and fifty dollars," Mrs. Cool interrupted. "Make it out to Bertha Cool. I'll send it down to the bank. If the check's any good, we'll find Morgan Birks. When we find him, we'll serve him. If we find him tomorrow, it costs you a hundred and fifty bucks. If it takes more than seven days, it costs you twenty dollars a day for every extra day we put in. No matter what happens, you get no refunds. Frankly, if we can't find him in seven days, I don't think we can ever find him. No use you throwing good money after bad. I'm telling you now."

"But you've *got* to find him," Alma Hunter said. "It's—it's imperative."

"Listen, dearie. The whole police force is trying to find him. I'm not saying we can't. I'm not saying we can. I'm just telling you how you can keep costs down."

"But the police force doesn't have Sandra helping them. Sandra can—"

"Do you mean that Sandra knows where he is?"

"No, but her brother does."

"Who's her brother?"

"His name's Thoms, B. Lee Thoms. He's going to help Sandra. She's at the train, meeting him. He knows who Morgan's girl friend is. You should be able to locate him through the girl friend."

Bertha Cool said, "All right. As soon as you get the money, we start."

Alma Hunter raised her purse. "I'll give you cash right now."

"How'd you happen to come to me?"

"Sandra's lawyer said you'd get results, that you took cases that the other detective agencies wouldn't touch—divorce cases and things of that sort, and—"

"Who in hell is he?" Bertha Cool interrupted. "I forgot to look at his name. Donald, hand me those papers—no, never mind, just read me the name of the lawyer."

I looked down at the bottom of the jacket. "Sydney Coltas," I said. "He has his office in the Temple Building."

"Never heard of him," Mrs. Cool said. "But he seems to know me. Sure I do anything—divorces, politics—anything. My idea of ethics in this business is cash and carry."

Alma Hunter said, "You did some work for a friend of his once."

Bertha Cool said, "Well, don't get me wrong, dearie. *I'm* not going to serve your summons. *I* don't go wandering around the highways and byways with papers in my hand. I hire people to do my leg work. Donald Lam is one of my legs."

The phone rang. She frowned and said, "I wish somebody'd invent a muzzle for a telephone so the damn thing wouldn't always ring in the middle of a sentence. Hello—hello, what is it? Yes, what do you want, Elsie? . . . All right, I'll put her on."

She pushed the telephone over to the corner of the desk, and said, "It's a call for you, Alma. A woman's on the line. Says it's an emergency."

Alma Hunter walked swiftly around the desk, picked up the telephone, put the receiver to her ear, gulped once, and said, "Hello."

The receiver rattled into noise. I saw Alma Hunter's face twist in a spasm of expression. She said, "For God's sake," and listened some more, then asked, "Where are you now? . . . Yes. . . . And you're going home from there. . . . Well, I'll meet you there. I'll come right away, just as quick as I can. . . . Yes, she's assigning a detective to work on the case— no—no, not herself. . . . No, she doesn't go out by herself. She's—she's—hardly—"

Bertha Cool said, "Don't be bashful. Tell her I'm fat."

"She's—well, she's fat," Alma Hunter said. "No, not that. Fat. F-a-t. . . . Yes, that's right. . . . No, he's a young man. All right, I'll bring him with me. How soon? All right—hold the phone a minute."

She looked up from the telephone and asked me, "Can you

go with me right away? That is, can Mrs. Cool let you start right now?"

It was Bertha Cool who answered. "Yes," she said, "you can do anything you want to with him, dearie. Put him on a collar and lead him around with a leash, for all I care. You've rented him. He's yours."

"Yes, I'll bring him," Alma Hunter said into the telephone, and hung up. She looked at Mrs. Cool. Her voice had just the suspicion of a quaver.

"That was Sandra," she announced. "She met her brother at the train, and someone ran into her automobile. Her brother was thrown through the windshield. She's at the emergency hospital. She says her brother knows all about the girl Morgan has been going with, but for some reason he doesn't want to tell. She says we'll have to put pressure on him."

Bertha Cool said, "Go ahead. Donald will know how to bring pressure to bear. He'll figure it out. Handle it any way you want. Only remember, if we find him tomorrow, it costs you a hundred and fifty bucks just the same."

"I understand," Miss Hunter said, "and I'll pay you now, if you please."

"I please," Bertha Cool said calmly.

Alma Hunter opened her purse, took out bills, and started counting them. While she was doing that, I glanced through the allegations of the divorce complaint. After all, those things are largely a matter of form, the allegation of the residence, of the marriage, the statistical statement necessary for the state bureau, the setting up of the cause of action, and the allegations on which alimony is predicated.

I skimmed through the unessential parts to concentrate on

the paragraph dealing with the cause for divorce. It was cruelty. Her husband had hit and slapped her, had on one occasion pushed her out of an automobile when she was a little slow in getting to the sidewalk, had called her "bitch" and "whore" in the presence of witnesses, all of which had caused her great and grievous mental suffering and physical anguish.

I looked up, to find Bertha Cool staring at me with gray eyes in which the pupils had contracted until they were black pinpoints. The currency lay uncounted on the blotter in front of her.

"Aren't you going to count it?" Alma Hunter asked.

"No," Mrs. Cool said. She scooped the money into a drawer, picked up the telephone, and said to Elsie Brand, "When Alma Hunter goes out, give her a receipt made to Sandra Birks for one hundred and fifty dollars."

She hung up the telephone and said to Alma Hunter, "That's all."

Alma Hunter got up and looked at me. I left the office with her. Elsie Brand had a receipt ready. She tore it from the receipt book, handed it to Alma Hunter, and turned back to her typewriter.

Alma Hunter looked across at me as we gained the corridor and started down toward the elevator. "I want to talk with you," she said.

I nodded.

"And please understand me. I know how you're feeling. After what Mrs. Cool said about having rented you, you feel like a gigolo or a poodle dog or something."

"Thanks," I said.

"Sandra told me the doctor would be patching her brother up for almost an hour, and not to come until he was finished."

"And you decided to kill that hour talkng to me?" I asked.

"Yes."

The light over the elevator shaft glowed red. "Is it too early for lunch?" she asked.

I thought of my twenty-five-cent breakfast and followed her into the elevator.

"No," I said.

CHAPTER THREE

WE SAT in a little, quiet restaurant down on a side street, a little place run by a big German woman. It was a new one on me. Alma Hunter said Sandra had been eating there for five or six months. The food was wonderful.

"Tell me—how long have you been working there?" Alma asked.

"You mean at the detective agency?"

"Yes, of course."

I said, "About three hours."

"I thought so. And you've been out of work for a while?"

"Yes."

"How in the world did a man of your size decide to become—er—that is—what experience have you had—or perhaps I shouldn't ask that."

"You shouldn't," I said.

She was silent for a moment, then said, "I'm going to give you some money for the lunch check. We'll do that on all meals we eat together. I don't want to put you in the position of standing by while I pay the check. As a man, you'll naturally resent—"

"Don't worry about me," I grinned. "All the pride I ever had has been kicked out of me. You've seen that for yourself."

"You mustn't be like that," she protested. Her eyes showed hurt.

"Ever walked the streets," I asked, "hungry—not able to talk to anyone, because the people you know would cut you and the people you didn't know would think you wanted a handout? Have you ever been counted out without having had any sort of a trial?"

"No," she said, "I don't think I have."

"Try it some time," I said. "It does a lot for your pride."

"You mustn't let it get you down."

"Oh no, it hasn't," I assured her politely.

"Now you're being sarcastic," she said. "I don't think, Mr.— I'm going to call you Donald. You call me Alma. When people are mixed up in a game such as we're mixed up in, it seems foolish to stand on a lot of formality."

"Tell me about the game we're mixed up in," I invited.

There was a queer expression in her eyes, a pleading perhaps, perhaps a loneliness, and, I thought, just a glint of fear.

"Tell me, Donald, and tell me the truth. You haven't had any previous experience as a detective, have you?"

I squeezed the last drops of coffee out of the coffee pot, and said, "Lovely weather we're having, isn't it?"

"That's what I thought."

"What is?"

She smiled. "That we're having lovely weather."

"That makes it unanimous," I observed.

"I didn't mean to hurt your feelings, Donald."

"You haven't. My feelings don't get hurt."

She leaned forward across the table. "I want you to help me, Donald."

"You heard what Mrs. Cool told you," I said, "that you

could put me on a collar and lead me around on a leash if you wanted to."

"Oh, Donald, *please* don't be like that. I understand how you must have felt. But don't take it out on me."

"I'm not. I'm trying to tell you that this is a business arrangement."

"I want it to be personal as well—you're hired to serve papers on Morgan Birks, but there are a lot of things about the case you should understand, and—and I want you to help me a little bit."

"Go on," I said, "it's your party."

She said, "Morgan was mixed up in this slot-machine business right up to his ears. It's a sordid story. There's graft, bribery, and corruption. Those machines were all adjusted so there was a terrific pay-off. They had to be. Morgan had to take care of the police. The places that leased them had to be given a big profit."

"Nothing particularly unusual about that, is there?"

"I don't know," she said. "It's my first experience with anything of the kind. I was shocked—and Sandra's changed a lot."

"Since when?"

"Since two years ago."

"Is that when she was married? In other words, since her marriage?"

"Yes."

"Did you know Morgan Birks before they were married?"

"No. I've never met him. He didn't like me."

"Why?"

"I think Sandra used me as a scapegoat. She wrote me long letters after they were married. You see, she was married on her vacation. She'd been saving her money for three years to make a trip to Honolulu. She met Morgan on the boat. They were married in Honolulu. She sent a wire giving up her job."

"What were you a scapegoat for?"

"Oh, lots of things," she evaded.

"Such as what? What's wrong with the way she acts?"

"Oh, around men. I guess Morgan's old-fashioned in his ideas, and I guess he's horribly jealous. He tells Sandra she's nothing but an exhibitionist."

"Is she?"

"No, of course not. Sandra's frank and modern and—well, she doesn't have any old-fashioned modesty about her body."

"Didn't Morgan Birks know that before he married her?"

She smiled and said, "Men like women to be modern with them. It's when they're modern with other men that the trouble starts."

"And Sandra blamed you?" I asked.

"No. But I think Morgan did. He thought someone had undermined Sandra's feeling about—well, about things like that, and because she'd been rooming with me, Morgan thinks I'm responsible."

"And how has Sandra changed?"

"I don't know. She's grown sort of hard and watchful and shrewd and calculating. She looks at you, and you get the feeling that she's hiding behind her eyes."

"When did you notice this?"

"As soon as I saw her again."

"And when was that?"

"About a week ago when this thing broke. She wrote and asked me to come and stay with her for a while."

"You're working?" I asked.

"No—not now. I burnt my bridges. I gave up my job to come and live with Sandra for a while."

"Do you think that was wise?"

"She told me I could get another job here."

"Where had you been working?"

"Kansas City."

"And that was where you met Sandra—where you roomed together?"

"No. Sandra and I were rooming together in Salt Lake City. She met Morgan on that Honolulu trip and never even came back for her things. I sent them on to her at Kansas City. Then, after a while, Morgan left and came here, and I drifted back East and had a job in Kansas City, but I wasn't there while Morgan was and—at least I don't think I was. I didn't keep up with Sandra. Morgan, you see, goes to places, stays there for a while, and then gets kicked out. Things get hot for him—well, like they are here, only this is the worst it's ever been."

The big German woman came to beam down at us and ask if we wanted any more coffee. Alma said, "No." I said, "Yes." She took my coffee pot away to fill it, and I said to Alma, "I'm doing about as much talking as you are. If you want to tell me things, why not go ahead and tell them?"

"What," she asked, "did you want to know?"

"Everything."

"I used to be simply crazy about Sandra," Alma said. "I guess I still am, but marriage has changed her a lot, all right, that and the sort of life she's lived with Morgan Birks." She laughed nervously and said, "I guess you think it's a scream. Morgan blaming me for the things he doesn't like in Sandra, and I claiming that Morgan has been responsible for a change in Sandra. I—"

"For God's sake," I said, "tell me the truth. What's the matter with Sandra? Is she on the make?"

"You couldn't blame her if she was," Alma said hotly. "Morgan never has been true to her. Within the first few months after her marriage, she found out he was keeping a mistress. It's been like that ever since."

"The same girl?" I asked.

"No. He couldn't even be true to a mistress."

"Well, according to your ideas," I said, "that's because Sandra didn't make a home for him, didn't—"

"Donald," she interrupted, "don't be like that. Now stop it."

The German woman brought my coffee. I said, "All right, I'm stopped, but you do think it's about six of one and a half a dozen of the other, don't you?"

"Morgan threw Sandra in with a wild crowd," she said. "He associates with gamblers and men of that type, and occasionally there'd be some politician he'd want Sandra to play up to. He'd keep telling her, 'My God, don't be so stiff. Go ahead and use a little sex appeal on this guy. I want him to like you. He's important to us.' He was after Sandra all the time to be sort of a glamour girl."

"All right," I said, "she's your friend. You won't say anything against her. There's no use wasting time trying to argue about it. Now, go ahead and tell me the rest of it."

"The rest of what?"

"The rest of what's worrying you."

"I think she's got some money that belongs to Morgan Birks."

"Where did she get it?"

"It's pay-off money. I think there were some safety deposit boxes in her name, or perhaps she'd an assumed name for those boxes. Morgan gave her money to put in there—I think it was money he had been given for bribery or something. I don't know. But anyhow, Sandra doesn't intend to let him get that money back."

"I take it," I said, "that when she plays marbles, she plays for keeps."

"Well, can you blame her?" Alma Hunter asked.

"I don't know," I said, "yet."

"Well, what I'm trying to tell you is that I'm afraid."

"Of what?"

"Of everything."

"Of Morgan Birks?"

"Yes."

"And is Sandra afraid of him?"

"No, and that's what bothers me. I think she should be."

"Did you read the divorce complaint?"

"Yes."

"Did you notice that she was trying to grab everything in sight? She wants to cash in on the life insurance, have a receiver appointed for the property, collect temporary alimony and attorney's fees, have a share of the community property awarded to her, and an allowance by way of alimony."

"That's what the lawyer put in. Lawyers always do that."

"Is that what Sandra told you?"

"Yes."

"And what do you want me to do?"

"You're right about Sandra; when she starts fighting, she

fights," she said. "She was always that way. One night a boy friend wasn't going to go home. He got rough, and Sandra was going to hit him with one of her golf clubs. She'd have done it, too."

"What stopped her?"

"I did."

"What happened to the boy friend?"

"He was frightened. I talked him into going home. He wasn't a friend, just an acquaintance."

"All right. Go on."

"Well, Sandra acts as though she were keeping something back from me, and I'm afraid she is. I think she's trying to take some advantage of Morgan. I don't know just how or what, and—well, I want you to find out and see what you can do to make her—well, be reasonable."

"And that's all?" I asked.

"Yes."

"How about you? Wasn't there something you wanted?"

She looked at me appraisingly for a moment, then slowly shook her head and said, "No."

I finished my coffee. "Go right ahead," I said. "Keep on thinking that I'm a babe in the woods who shouldn't be trusted out alone after dark. You know damn well that if I'd told you I had two or three years as a detective back of me, you'd have told me what's really on your mind. The way it is now, you figure I can't be trusted."

She started to say something then, but checked herself just as she started to speak.

"Go ahead," I said. "Pay the check, and let's go meet the brother, and see what he has to say."

"And you won't tell anyone what I've told you?"

"You haven't told me anything—what did you say the brother's name was?"

"Thoms."

"His first name?"

"I don't think I've ever heard it. It's B. Lee Thoms. That's the way he signs his name. Sandra calls him Bleatie. She always has."

I motioned to the German woman to bring us the check, and said, "Let's go see Bleatie."

CHAPTER FOUR

IF ALMA Hunter had a key to the apartment, she didn't use it. She stood in the hallway and jabbed her gloved thumb against the buzzer at the side of the door. The young woman who opened the door and stood looking out at us was in the late twenties. She was slender around the waist, but had curves, and her dress showed the curves. Her hair was black. Her eyes were big, dark, and expressive. She had high cheekbones and very red, full lips. Her eyes veered away from Alma Hunter to study me, as though I'd been a new horse brought home from the fair.

Alma Hunter said, "Sandra, this is Donald Lam. He works for Bertha Cool's agency. And he's going to find Morgan and serve the papers on him. Tell me about the accident. Was it bad?"

Sandra Birks looked at me with surprised eyes. "You don't look like a detective," she said, and gave me her hand.

She didn't just extend her hand. She didn't shake hands, but she gave me her hand just exactly as though she were turning over a part of her body to me.

As I closed my fingers around her hand, it surrendered in mine. "I try to look innocent," I said.

"I'm *so* glad you came, Mr. Lam," she said, laughing nervously. "It's imperative that we find Morgan at once. I think you understand why— Come in."

I stood to one side and let Alma Hunter walk in first. It was a big room, with dark beams across the ceiling, heavy drapes across the windows, thick carpets underfoot. Lounging chairs were scattered about, with cigarettes and ash trays handy. It was a place that reeked with the feeling of having been lived in, a sensual, human, warm existence.

Sandra Birks said, "Archie's here. I was fortunate to get him—I don't think you've ever met Archie, have you, Alma?"

"Archie?" Alma repeated with the rising inflection of one who asks a question.

"Archie Holoman. You know, Dr. Holoman. He was just graduating when I was married. He's in a hospital and isn't supposed to take outside cases, but of course Bleatie is different. It's all part of the family."

I saw from the way Alma smiled and nodded that she'd never heard of Archie before, and gathered that Sandra had a trick of producing intimate men friends just as a magician takes rabbits out of a hat.

"Do sit down," Sandra Birks said to me. "I'm going to see if Bleatie can talk. It was the most *awful* thing! That car swung around the corner and banged into me before I had an opportunity to do anything. Bleatie swears the driver did it on purpose. It was a big, old car, and it got away. I hung onto the steering wheel. Bleatie lunged forward and went right through the windshield. The doctor says his nose is broken. I didn't know that when I telephoned you, Alma. . . . Do sit down, Mr. Lam. Pick a comfortable chair, stretch out, and have a cigarette. I want to talk with Alma for a minute."

I dropped into a chair, put my feet up on an ottoman, lit

a cigarette, and blew smoke rings at the ceiling. Bertha Cool was getting twenty dollars a day for my time. My stomach had food.

From a bedroom I could hear the sounds of motion, the rumble of a masculine voice, then a ripping sound as adhesive tape was torn in strips. I could hear Sandra Birks talk rapidly in a low monotone. Occasionally Alma interrupted with a question. After a while, they came back and Mrs. Birks said, "I want you to talk with my brother."

I ground out my cigarette, followed them on into the bedroom. A young chap with a triangular face, broad across the forehead and eyes, coming down to a weak point at the chin, was putting on bandages with a professional touch. A man lay on the bed, cursing every now and then in a low voice. His nose was built up with splints, bandage, and adhesive tape. His long black hair was parted in the middle and hung down on either side of a sloping forehead. There was a bald spot about two inches in diameter on the top of his head. The adhesive tape, radiating out from the bandages on his nose made it seem as though his eyes were peering out from behind a white, coarse spiderweb.

The man's body was heavier than one would have gathered from looking at his face. His stomach bulged prominently against his vest. His hands were small, the fingers long and tapering. I judged that he was probably five or six years older than his sister.

Sandra Birks said, "This is the man who's going to serve the papers on Morgan, Bleatie."

He looked at me then, a peculiarly disconcerting stare from cat-green eyes on either side of the bandaged beak. "For Christ's sake!" he said, and then, after a moment, "What's his name?"

And the way his voice came through the bandages made it sound as though he'd said, "Whad's hid nabe?"

"Donald Lam," I told him.

"I want to talk with you," he said.

"I wish you would," Sandra chimed in. "You know time's precious. Morgan may leave the country any time."

"He won't leave the country without me knowing it," Bleatie said. "Look here, Doctor, how about it? Are you finished?"

The young doctor cocked his head on one side as a sculptor might survey a finished masterpiece.

"You'll get by now," he said, "but no sudden exertion, nothing which will run up a quick blood pressure and start a hemorrhage. For three or four days take a mild laxative. Take your temperature every four hours. If you start running a fever, get in touch with me at once."

"All right," Bleatie said. "Get out, the whole outfit of you. I've got something to say to Lam. Go on, Sandra, and you too, Alma. Go have a drink. Beat it."

They went out like a bunch of chickens being shooed out of a garden patch. Before the blast of that dominating personality, the doctor lost his paternal sick-room manner and scuttled out through the door along with the rest. When the door was closed, the green eyes turned once more to me. "Are you with a lawyer?" he asked.

I had some difficulty understanding his conversation at first. He talked like a man with a clothespin clamped over his nose. "No," I said, "I'm with a bureau of investigation."

"How well do you know Sandra?" There was suspicion in his eyes, a suspicion which, for the moment, I couldn't understand.

"I met her for the first time about five minutes ago."

"What do you know about her?"

"Nothing except what Miss Hunter told me."

"What did she tell you?"

"Nothing."

"She's my sister," Bleatie said, "and I should stick up for her, but God knows she has her faults, and they're a pretty important element in this whole mess. If you ask me, she's given her husband a hell of a raw deal. She can't be trusted around a man. She's never happy unless she has half a dozen men on the string, playing one of them against the other. She's married, but marriage doesn't stop her a damn bit. She goes her own way, and does pretty much as she pleases."

"They all do these days," I said easily.

"You seem to be rushing to her defense a little too eagerly—considering that you've only known her a few minutes," he said.

I kept quiet.

"You're sure you're not lying to me."

"I'm not accustomed to lie to anyone," I said, "and I don't like to have people with broken noses accuse me of being a liar."

He grinned then. I could see the cheek muscles twist and the eyes narrow. "Sort of taking an unfair advantage, is it?" he asked.

"Yes. You can't hit a man with a busted nose."

"I don't know why not," he said. "*I* wouldn't hesitate."

I looked into the cat-green eyes and said thoughtfully, "No, I don't suppose you would."

"If a man's nose is broken, that makes him all the more vulnerable. When I fight, I don't spar for points. I fight to smash the other man, and the harder I can smash him, the better I like it. And you're a little shrimp to have such a game-cock disposition."

He'd have liked me to make some comment then. I didn't make any.

"So Sandra wants a divorce, does she?" he said after a moment.

"So I understand."

"Well, there's a hell of a lot to be said on Morgan's side of this thing. Has that ever occurred to you?"

"I'm serving the papers," I said. "He'll have a chance to tell his side of it in court."

"The hell he will!" Bleatie said impatiently. "How the devil could he come into court? He's a fugitive from justice. Hell, they'd rip him wide open. What's all the big rush about? Why doesn't Sandra serve him by publication?"

"It would take too long," I said, "and you can't collect alimony on a service by publication."

"She wants alimony?" he asked, then added quickly, "Thought you said you weren't a lawyer."

"I think you'll have to ask her or her lawyer about the alimony," I said. "After all, I'm only hired to serve the papers."

"You have the papers there?"

"Yes."

"Let's see 'em."

I passed the papers over. He hunched around on the bed, said, "Put your hand behind my shoulders and give me a boost—there, that's better—now get that pillow down—you probably think I'm a hell of a brother, but we're not a particularly conventional family—and when you come right down to it, I don't give a *damn* what you think."

"I'm not paid to think," I said. "I'm paid to serve papers. And if you want to be personal, I don't give a damn what *you* think."

"That's good. I like your spunk. Sit down there and don't interrupt me for a minute."

He took the papers, glanced through the summons, and read

through the divorce complaint with the laborious thoroughness of a layman who isn't familiar with legal papers and has to puzzle through all the whereases, whyfores, and aforesaids. When he had finished, he folded the papers and handed them back to me. His eyes were narrowed thoughtfully. "So she wants a court order giving her the custody of the contents of all of the safety deposit boxes, does she?"

"All I know is what's in the papers," I said. "You've read those now. You know as much as I do."

"Pretty cagey, aren't you?" he asked.

"I'm paid to serve papers," I said. "Why don't you talk with your sister if you want to find out just what she has in mind?"

"Don't worry," he said grimly, "I'm going to."

"Do you," I asked, "know where her husband is?"

"I know Morgan's mistress," he said simply, "and she's a damn nice girl."

"Mrs. Birks could have dragged her into the case," I pointed out. "She didn't."

He laughed, and his laugh wasn't pleasant. "A fat chance she'd have, dragging anyone into the case," he said. "My God, you don't know women very well, if you can't size Sandra up just by looking at her."

He was talking about his sister. I kept quiet.

"If you're ever left alone in the room with her for ten minutes, she'll make a pass at you—oh, don't look so shocked about it."

"I'm not shocked."

"Well, I'm warning you. We're an unconventional family. Hell, I don't hold it against her. She lives her life. I live mine. But she's a shrewd, selfish, scheming vixen. She has the morals of a cat. She's attractive as hell. She has a quick mind—and she uses it most of the time to get something she wants—Hell, I should talk things over with *you*. Tell her to come in here."

I stepped to the door and said, "Mrs. Birks, your brother wants to talk with you."

"You want me to clear out?" I asked.

"Hell, no. I want you in here."

I moved over to the side of the bed. Sandra Birks came in, and said, anxiously, "What is it, Bleatie? Are you feeling all right now? The doctor left this sedative to give you if you get nervous and—"

"Nix on that God damn cooing," Bleatie said. "You always did put on that solicitous air when you wanted something. Christ Almighty, I'm your brother. I know you like a book. I know what you want. You want to get the name of Morgan's girl out of me. You want to serve papers on Morgan. You want to get a divorce. You want to be free to marry your latest sweetie. Who is he? That young squirt of a doctor? I've got my suspicions about him."

"Bleatie!" she said. "Don't!" and glanced apprehensively at me. "You mustn't talk that way. You've been through a nervous shock, and you're upset and—"

"Upset, hell!" he interrupted. "Any time a man can't be twisted around your fingers, it's because he's upset and isn't himself—well, I don't blame you. Now look here, Sandra. You and I are going to have a showdown. You're my sister. I suppose I should be loyal to you. It also happens that I'm a friend of Morgan Birks. Just because he's down at the moment, is no sign you're going to jump on him with both feet."

"Who wants to jump on him with both feet?" she countered, her eyes beginning to glint. "I've given him all of the breaks in that divorce complaint. My God, the things I *could* have said about him would—"

"Wouldn't have done you a damn bit of good," Bleatie said. "Think of the things Morgan could say about *you*. Look at you! You never can forget your sex. I get my nose busted and damned if you don't have to drag in your current boy friend—or one of your current boy friends—to practice on me. That young squirt ain't dry behind the ears yet, and you drag him in—"

"Bleatie! You stop," she said. "Archie Holoman is a fine young man. Morgan knows him. He's a friend of the family. There's absolutely nothing between us."

His laugh was cynical. "So Morgan knows him, does he? And he's a friend of the family? You know what *that* means? Just because he comes to the house and shakes hands with your husband and smokes his cigars, makes him a friend of the family, does it? How about the times you see him when Morgan ain't around?"

"Bleatie," she said, "you cut that out or *I'll* start doing a little talking. You're no tin angel yourself. You make me sick with this holier-than-thou attitude. If you want to sling mud, I'll scoop up a handful. That little—"

He held up his hand and said, "Keep your shirt on, baby, keep your shirt on. I'm just leading up to something."

"Well, lead up to it right now."

"I'll give you a chance at Morgan," he said. "You can serve those papers on him and go ahead and rush your divorce case through. But I'm going to see that Morgan has a square deal."

"What do you want?"

"That whole paragraph in there about property," he said. "You were earning your living when Morgan met you. You've feathered your nest since then. God knows how much you've picked up, but it's plenty—you and that wheedling, cooing way of yours. You've managed to get a pretty good apartment here. I suppose the rent is paid for a while on a lease. You've got a whole closet full of glad rags. You've salted a nice little wad of dough. With those clothes on your back, your figure, and your knowledge of what it takes to make men putty in your hands, you'll take a trip to Europe and wind up with a couple of dukes."

"You showed him those papers?" she asked me, the words coming out in a rush. "You let him read my divorce complaint?"

"Yes," I said. "You sent me in to talk to him."

She said irritably, "Of all the fool things—" She broke off, turned to her brother. "I'm finished with men," she said.

He laughed sarcastically.

Sandra Birks had lightning in her eyes, but she kept her voice calm. "What do you want, Bleatie? This isn't getting us anywhere."

"I want you to go to your lawyer and get a new divorce complaint. I want one that doesn't have anything in it about property. You get a divorce. You go your way; Morgan goes his. That's fair."

"What do you mean, property?"

"That stuff about the safety deposit boxes and all that stuff. You—"

She whirled on me. "You're responsible for this. Why did you think you had to show him the papers?"

"I made him," Bleatie said. "Keep your shirt on, Babe. I wasn't going to be a sucker in this thing. One of these days Morgan is going to be out in the clear. Morgan can look me up then. Morgan isn't a damn fool. The minute I drag the girl into it, he's going to know where the tip-off came from. Remember that—Morgan Birks *isn't anybody's damn fool!*"

"I haven't any time to go to my lawyers and get another complaint," she said. "This one has already been filed and a summons issued."

"Well, you can change it, can't you?"

"I don't think so."

"Sit down there at that desk," he said, "and write a letter. Put in that letter that you're asking for property in your divorce complaint, but you really don't want any, that when the case comes up for trial, you'll have your lawyer tell the judge you don't want alimony, that you'll keep the apartment for as long as the rent is paid, that you'll keep your clothes and whatever money you have in your jeans, and Morgan can have all the rest."

"What are you going to do with that letter?" she asked.

"See that you give Morgan a square deal."

Her mouth was a firm, straight line. Her eyes were hot with anger. The man on the bed met her gaze with the calm assurance of one who is so accustomed to having people yield that he doesn't even take the possibility of their disobedience into consideration. After a second or two, she walked over to the desk, jerked open the drawer as though she were going to pull it out by the roots, yanked out a sheet of paper, and wrote.

Bleatie said to me, "God knows how a cigarette will taste, but I'm going to try one anyway. You got one?"

I nodded.

"Put it in my mouth," he said, "and light it for me, will you? The way this bandage sticks out on my nose, I'd probably burn the side of my face off trying to find the end of the cigarette."

I gave him the cigarette and lit it. He inhaled a couple of deep drags and said, "God, it tastes funny!"

After that, he smoked in silence. Over at the desk, Sandra Birks scratched the pen across the paper. When an inch of the cigarette had burned down, she finished writing, blotted the paper, read it over, and handed it across to her brother. "All right," she said. "Now I hope you're satisfied. You'd strip your own sister naked just to give a lousy friend a break."

He read it through twice, then said, "I think that's all right." He folded the paper, fumbled around until he found his pants pocket, and pushed it down inside. He looked up at me and said, "Okay, buddy. Do your stuff. The girl is Sally Durke. She lives in the Milestone Apartments. Go up there and get hard with her. Get plenty hard. You've got to spread it on thick. Throw a good scare into her. Tell her she's hiding Morgan, that you're going to see she's arrested for harboring a fugitive from justice or whatever kind of a stall you want to make. Tell her that Sandra is suing for divorce, is going to drag her into it and is out to collect all Morgan's property. Don't say a word to her about this letter Sandra has given me. Pretend you're a cop—no, you'd never make that stick—but get hard."

"Then what?" I asked.

"Then shadow her. She'll lead you to Morgan."

"Morgan won't come there?"

"Hell, no. Morgan's too smart for that. Morgan keeps in touch with her, but he isn't fool enough to walk into a trap like that, not when he knows the cops are looking for him."

I turned to Sandra Birks. "Got some good pictures of your husband?" I asked.

"Yes," she said.

Bleatie said, "You'll find his pictures in the newspapers."

"I know," I agreed, "but they're no good. I've already checked up on them."

"I have a couple of snapshots and a good photographic portrait," Sandra said.

"I'd prefer the snapshots."

"Will you come this way, please?"

I nodded to Bleatie.

"Good luck, Lam," he said, and stretched out on the bed. His lips looked as though he wanted to grin and couldn't. "When you get done, Sandra, come back and give me that sedative. I think in about half an hour this nose is going to be hurting like hell—it's a wonder you couldn't watch where you're driving."

"Watch where I'm driving," she said. "My God, that's just like you. At the time, you claimed the other car deliberately ran into us. If you could only stay put once—"

"Save it," he said. "Lam isn't interested in the brotherly and sisterly affection of the Thoms family."

Her eyes glared cold daggers at him. "It took you a hell of a while to find *that* out," she said, and flounced out of the room. I followed along behind, closing the door after me.

Alma Hunter looked up with apprehensive eyes. "Did you get it?" she asked breathlessly.

Sandra Birks nodded grimly. "You *bet* I got it," she said in a low voice, "and what I'm going to do to *that* baby isn't even going to be funny!"

She kept on walking right through the living room and across to a bedroom. "Come in here, Mr. Lam," she invited.

There were twin beds, pictures on the walls. The furniture was expensive, with plate-glass mirrors at various angles of the room. She said, "I have a photograph album here in my dresser drawer. Sit down over there—maybe you'd better sit on the bed because I'll want to sit beside you. We'll go over the photographs together, and you can pick out the ones you want."

I sat down on the bed. She opened a drawer in the dresser,

took out a photograph album, and came over and sat down beside me.

"What was my brother telling you about me?" she asked, holding the album unopened.

"Nothing much."

"Yes he did. He—he has a nasty mind. I don't care if he *is* my own brother."

"We," I reminded, "were to get a picture of your husband. Is it here?"

She made a little face by wrinkling her nose, and said, "Don't, by any chance, forget whom you're working for."

"I won't."

"Well?" she asked.

I raised my eyebrows in a silent question.

"I'm waiting to hear what Bleatie had to say about me."

"Nothing much."

"Did he say I was selfish?"

"I don't remember exactly how he expressed it."

"Did he say that I was sex-crazy?"

"No."

"Well," she said, bitterly, "he's improving. He usually has that idea about me. My God, I wouldn't put it past him to even claim Dr. Holoman was a lover."

When I didn't say anything, she let her eyes glitter at me from under half-lowered lids. "Well," she asked, "did he?"

"Was that what you really wanted to know?" I inquired.

"Of course I want to know."

"Just what is it you want to know?"

"What did Bleatie suspect—did he accuse me of being friendly with Dr. Holoman?"

"I can't remember."

"Your memory isn't very good, is it?"

"No."

"Perhaps you wouldn't make a good detective."

"Perhaps."

"You're working for me, you know."

"I'm working for a woman by the name of Bertha L. Cool," I said. "I make my reports directly to her. As I understand it, I'm employed to serve papers on Morgan Birks; and I gather that you brought me in here to show me some photographs of your husband."

"You're being impertinent."

"I'm sorry."

"Oh well," she said, "I don't know why I'm so crazy as to want an answer. I know what the answer is. Of course, he panned me. We never did care for each other as brother and sister are supposed to care. But I didn't think that even he would drag Dr. Holoman into it."

"I'd prefer snapshots," I said, "that show the face with some sort of expression, laughing or smiling."

She almost threw the album into my lap.

She opened the book. I started turning pages.

The first picture was of Sandra Birks seated on a rustic bench with a waterfall in back, pine trees, and a stream running across the left foreground. A man had his arm around her shoulders. She was looking up into his eyes.

"That Morgan?" I asked.

"No," she said, and turned the page.

She turned the leaves rapidly. "I don't know just where it is," she apologized. "I put these pictures in helter-skelter. We were on a vacation trip together and—" She turned two more pages, said, "There he is," and leaned across me to point.

It was a good clear photograph of a tall, thin man with sharp features, glossy black hair combed straight back away from a high forehead.

"That," I told her, "is exactly what I want. It's a clear picture. Got any others?"

She slid the pointed tips of her crimson nails under the picture, lifted it from the corners by which it was fastened to the book. "Perhaps," she said.

She turned two or three pages—pages that were filled with ordinary photographs, people in cars, people sitting on porches, people grinning inanely at the camera. Then she said, "Here are three or four pages taken on our vacation. Some of us girls went swimming together—you mustn't look."

She peeked down into the pages, giggled, turned four or five of them all at once, and then found another picture of her husband. "This isn't quite as good as the other," she said, "but it gives you a profile view."

I took it, compared it with the other, and said, "This is fine. Thanks."

"Are those all you need?"

"Yes."

She continued to sit there on the bed, her lips slightly parted, her eyes focused on distance as though thinking something over. Abruptly she said, "Excuse me for a minute. There's something I want to ask Alma."

She jumped up from the bed and went out into the other room, leaving me holding the photograph album. I tossed it up to the head of the bed.

She was gone a couple of minutes. When she came back, Alma was with her.

"I thought perhaps you'd like to have one of the newspaper pictures," Sandra Birks said. "Here it is."

She'd clipped a picture from a newspaper. The caption read: "MORGAN BIRKS, ALLEGED PAY-OFF MAN FOR SLOT-MACHINE SYNDICATE, WHOSE PRESENCE IS SOUGHT BEFORE THE GRAND JURY."

I compared the picture with the two photographs. The newspaper picture wasn't clear but was quite evidently that of the man whose photograph I held.

Sandra Birks gave a little squeal and grabbed for the photograph book. "Oh, I forgot about this," she said.

Alma Hunter looked at her questioningly.

"It has those swimming pictures in it," she said, and laughed. "I left Mr. Lam unchaperoned with them."

I said, "I didn't look. I'll take these pictures, report to Mrs. Cool, and get in touch with Sally Durke. You'd better give me your telephone number so I can call you as soon as I have something to report."

Sandra said, "One thing, Mr. Lam. I want to know exactly when the papers are going to be served."

"I'll report to Mrs. Cool as soon as I've made the service," I said.

"That isn't what I want. I want to know about an hour *before* you serve the papers."

"Why?"

"I have reasons."

"What are they?"

"I think Bleatie may be planning to double-cross me."

"Orders," I said, "come through Mrs. Cool. You'll have to get in touch with her."

"Will you wait?" she asked.

"I'll stop by the office to report," I said.

"All right. Here, take my telephone number, and you, Alma, take my car and go with him. You can drive him around. It'll save time—you'll need a car, Mr. Lam, if you're going to be shadowing this girl. I have an extra one you might just as well take. Do you drive?"

I looked at Alma. "I'd prefer a driver."

"You'll drive him, Alma? Do. There's a good girl."

Alma said, "I'll do anything I can to help. You know that, Sandra."

She walked across to the dressing table, patted her hair, powdered her face, and tilted back her head to apply lipstick. A stretch of her neck was visible above the high collar. I thought at first the reflected light from the mirror was throwing splotches of shadow on it. Then I saw they were dark spots—bruises.

Sandra Birks said quickly, "Well, let's go in the other room and let Alma dress."

"I don't want to dress," Alma Hunter said.

"I'll buy you a drink, Mr. Lam," Sandra Birks invited.

"No, thanks. I don't drink when I'm working."

"My, what a moral young man," she exclaimed, and her voice was mocking. "You have *no* vices."

"I'm working for you," I pointed out. "It's costing you money."

"Yes, that's right. I suppose you're to be commended." Her voice didn't sound as though she really thought so.

"Your brother," I reminded her, "wanted to have that sedative the doctor left."

"Oh, he can wait—the big baby—tell me, what did he say about me?" Her manner was teasing, coquettish. She was very much aware that she was a woman. "What did he say about Archie?"

Alma whirled away from the mirror to watch me with warning eyes.

"He said that he thought Dr. Holoman was a very skillful doctor," I said. "He told me you were impulsive and headstrong but as good as gold, that he didn't always agree with you on little things, but that you always pulled together on big things; that whenever you got in a jam of any kind you could call on him and he'd stand back of you to the limit."

"Did he tell you that?"

"That's what I gathered from his conversation."

She stood staring at me. Her eyes were round. There was an expression in them I couldn't exactly classify. For a moment, I thought it might be fear.

"Oh," she said.

Alma Hunter nodded to me. "Let's go," she said.

CHAPTER FIVE

IT LACKED five minutes to twelve when I reached the office. A sign on the door announced that no further applicants were being interviewed. There were still men coming in to answer the ad. Two of them were standing in front of the door reading the sign as I approached. They turned away and walked past me with the steady mechanical tread of soldiers retreating from a lost battle.

Elsie Brand had finished her typing. She was seated at the desk with the left-hand top drawer open. She closed it as I opened the door.

"What's the matter?" I asked. "Aren't you supposed to read a magazine in between times?"

Her eyes looked me over, a head-to-foot glance. Then she slowly opened the left-hand drawer of the desk, and started reading again. From where I was standing, I could see that it was one of the movie magazines.

"How about ringing our employer," I suggested, "and telling her that Operative Thirteen is in the outer office with a report to make?"

She looked up from the magazine. "Mrs. Cool's at lunch."

"When will she be back?"

"Noon."

I leaned across her desk. "Under those circumstances, I have five minutes to wait," I said. "Would you prefer to talk with me or read the magazine?"

She said, "Do you have anything worth while to talk about?"

I met her eyes, and said, "No."

For a moment, there was a faint flash of humor in her eyes. "I hate to listen to worth while conversations," she admitted. "That's a movie magazine in the drawer. I haven't read *The Citadel, Gone with the Wind,* or any other worth while books. What's more, I don't intend to. Now, what did you want to talk about?"

"Well," I said, "for a starter, how about discussing Mrs. Cool? What time does she go to lunch?"

"Eleven."

"And gets back at twelve? And you leave at twelve and get back at one?"

"Yes."

I saw she was quite a bit older than my first estimate. I had figured her then as being in the late twenties. Now, she could have been in the middle thirties. She'd taken care of her face and figure, but there was more than the suggestion of a line running down from her ears; and the crease under her chin, faint though it was, meant that she'd lived longer than the twenty-seven or twenty-eight years I'd given her on my first estimate.

"I have Alma Hunter waiting for me in a car at the curb," I said. "If Mrs. Cool isn't apt to be back on time, I'd better run down and tell her."

"She'll be back on time," Elsie Brand said, "at any rate, within two or three minutes after twelve. That's one thing about Bertha Cool. She believes a person is entitled to food, and she wouldn't keep you waiting on your lunch hour."

"She seems to be quite a character," I said tentatively.

"She is," Elsie Brand said.

"How'd she happen to get in the detective agency field?"

"Her husband died."

"There are lots of other things for a woman to go into to make a living," I said inanely.

"What, for instance?" she asked.

"She could have modeled gowns," I suggested. "How long have you been with her?"

"Ever since she opened up."

"And how long has that been?"

"Three years."

"Did you know her before her husband died?"

"I was her husband's secretary," she said. "Bertha got me the job with him. She—"

Elsie Brand broke off as she heard the sound of steps in the corridor. Then a shadow formed on the ground glass of the entrance door, and Bertha Cool flowed majestically into the room. "All right, Elsie," she said. "You may go now. What do *you* want, Donald?"

"I want to make a report."

"Come in," she said.

She strode into the private office shoulders back, breasts and hips swinging loosely inside her voluminous, thin dress. It was hot outside, but she didn't seem to mind the heat.

"Sit down," she said. "Have you located him yet?"

"Not the husband. I've talked with the brother."

"Well, get busy and locate him."

"I'm going to."

"Of course you are. How good are you at arithmetic?"

"What's the problem?" I asked.

"I've received a flat fee covering seven days' work. If you work seven days on this job, I make a hundred and fifty dollars. If you work one day on it, I make a hundred and fifty dollars. If you clean up the case today, I have six days of your time to peddle to some other client. Figure that out, and tell me the answer. You're not going to serve any papers hanging around this office. Get the hell out and serve those papers."

"I came by to make a report."

"I don't want any report. I want action."

"I may need someone to help me."

"What for?"

"I have to shadow a girl. I've located Morgan Birks' girl friend. I have to tell her something to make her run to Morgan and then shadow her."

"Well, what's holding you back?"

"I've arranged for a car. Miss Hunter is going to drive me."

"All right. Let her drive. One other thing," she said. "As soon as you get Morgan Birks located, call Sandra."

"That may interfere with the service of the papers," I said.

She grinned. "Don't worry about that. Financial arrangements have been duly and properly made."

"I may get into a mess. That's a screwy family. Sandra Birks' brother intimates there's more to be said on Birks' side of the case than on hers."

"We're not paid to take sides; we're paid to serve papers."

"I understand that, but there may be some trouble. How about giving me something to show I'm working for the agency?"

She looked at me for a moment, then opened a drawer in her desk, took out a printed form, and filled it in with my name, age, and description. She signed it, blotted it, and handed it to me.

"Now how about a gun?" I asked.

"No."

"I may get in a jam."

"No."

"Suppose I do?"

"Fight your way out."

"I can do a lot more with a gun," I said.

"You can do too much with a gun. You've been reading detective magazines."

I said, "You're the boss," and started for the door. She said, "Wait a minute. Come back here. While you're here, I have something to say."

I turned back.

"I've found out all about you, Donald," she said in a motherly tone of voice. "You gave yourself away the way you looked through those legal papers this morning. I knew right away you'd had a legal education. You're young. You've been in trouble. You weren't trying to get work in a law office. When I asked you about your education, you didn't dare to tell me anything about your law work."

I tried to keep my face under control.

"Donald," she said, "I know your real name. I know all about your trouble. You were admitted to the bar. You were disbarred for violating professional ethics."

"I wasn't disbarred," I said, "and I didn't violate professional ethics."

"The grievance committee reported that you did."

"The grievance committee were a lot of stuffed shirts. I talked too much, that's all."

"What about, Donald?"

"I did some work for a client," I said. "We got to talking about the law. I told him a man could break any law and get away with it if he went at it right."

"That's nothing," she said. "Anyone knows that."

"The trouble is I didn't stop there," I confessed. "I told you I liked to scheme. I don't figure knowledge is any good unless you can apply it. I'd studied out a lot of legal tricks. I knew how to apply them."

"Go on from there," she said, her eyes showing interest. "What happened?"

"I told this man it would be possible to commit a murder so there was nothing anyone could do about it. He said I was wrong. I got mad and offered to bet him five hundred dollars I was right, and could prove it. He said he was ready to put up the money any time I'd put up my five hundred bucks. I told him to come back the next day. That night he was arrested. He turned out to be a small-time gangster. He babbled everything he knew to the police. Among other things, he told them that I had agreed to tell him how he could commit a murder and get off scot-free. That he was to pay me five hundred dollars for the information, and then if it looked good to him, he had planned to bump off a rival gangster."

"What happened?" she asked.

"The grievance committee went after me hammer and tongs. They revoked my license for a year. They thought I was some sort of a shyster. I told them it was an argument and a bet. Under the circumstances, they didn't believe me. And, naturally, they took the other side of the question—that a man couldn't commit deliberate murder and go unpunished."

"Could he, Donald?" she asked.

"Yes," I said.

"And you know how?"

"Yes. I told you that was my weakness. I like to figure things out."

"And locked inside that head of yours is a plan by which I could kill someone and the law couldn't do a damn thing about it?"

"Yes."

"You mean if I was smart enough so I didn't get caught."

"I don't mean anything of the sort. You'd have to put yourself in my hands and do just as I told you."

"You don't mean that old gag about fixing it so they couldn't find the body?"

"That," I said, "is the bunk. I'm talking about a loophole in the law itself, something a man could take advantage of to commit a murder."

"Tell me, Donald."

I laughed and said, "Remember, I've been through that once."

"When's your year up?"

"It's up. It was up two months ago."

"Why aren't you back practicing law?"

"It takes money to fit up an office with furniture, law books, and wait for clients," I said.

"Won't the law-book companies trust you?"

"Not after you've been suspended."

"And you couldn't get a job in a law office?"

"Not a chance."

"What do you intend to do with your legal education, Donald?"

"Serve papers," I said, and turned on my heel. I walked out through the outer office. Elsie Brand had gone to lunch. Alma

Hunter was waiting for me in the car. "I had to use sex appeal on a traffic cop," she said.

"Good girl," I approved. "Let's go to the Milestone Apartments, and I'll do my stuff with Sally Durke."

She turned to look back through the window in the rear of the car, at the traffic. As she twisted her neck free of the high collar of the silk blouse, I saw once more those dark, sinister bruises—the imprints left by thumb and fingers which had clutched her throat.

I said nothing. I had plenty of thinking of my own to do. She deftly swung the car out into traffic and drove to the Milestone Apartments.

"Well," I said. "Here goes."

"Luck," she said with a smile.

"Thanks."

I walked across the street, looked over the list of names on the side of the door, and pressed the button opposite the name "S. L. Durke, 314."

I was wondering just what a competent operative would do if Miss Durke wasn't at home. But before I'd decided on an answer, the door buzzer indicated Miss Durke was home and was willing to see visitors without a palaver through the speaking tube.

I pushed the door as the buzzer released the catch, walked down a smelly corridor to where a patch of pale light marked the location of the automatic elevator. I closed the door, jabbed the button for the third floor, and went up.

As I raised my fingers to knock on the door of 314, a girl in dark blue silk pajamas opened the door, and said, "What is it?"

She was a blonde, and I figured her as an artificial blonde. She was somewhere on the sunny side of thirty, with a figure that pushed out at me through the silk of her pajamas. She said again, impatiently, "Well, what is it?"

Her voice was the only harsh thing about her.

"I want to come in."

"Why?"

"I want to talk."

"Well, come on in," she said.

She'd been polishing her finger nails. The buffer was on a coffee table near a couch. She walked back to the couch, made herself comfortable, picked up the buffer, critically inspected her nails, and said without looking up, "Well, what is it?"

"I'm a detective," I told her.

Her eyes flashed up at mine then. For a moment there was a startled look on her face. Then she started to laugh. She quit laughing at the look on my face, and said, "*You* are?"

I nodded.

"Well, you don't look it," she observed, trying to soften the blow of her laughter. "You look like a darn nice kid with ideals and a mother. I hope I didn't hurt your feelings by laughing."

"No, I'm used to it."

"All right. You're a detective. So what?"

"I'm employed by Sandra Birks. Does that mean anything to you?"

She kept her eyes on the buffer as she polished her nails, apparently giving rapt attention to getting just the right sheen. "What's Sandra Birks got to do with it?" she asked at length.

"She might have quite a good deal to do with it."

"I don't know the lady."

"She's the wife of Morgan Birks."

"Who's Morgan Birks?"

"Why, don't you read the newspapers?" I asked.

"What if I do? Where do *I* come into that picture?"

I said, "Mrs. Birks could be pretty mean if she wanted to, you know."

"Could she?"

"You know she could."

"And how am I supposed to know it?"

"Let your conscience be your guide."

She looked up at me and laughed harshly. "I haven't any. I had to get rid of that long ago."

"Mrs. Birks," I said, "could drag you into court if she wanted to."

"On what ground?"

"On the ground of being intimate with her husband."

"Don't you take a lot for granted?" she asked.

"I don't know. Do I?"

"Go ahead. You're talking. I'm listening—for a while."

"Well, I'm doing what I've been hired to do."

"And what's that?"

"Serve papers on Morgan Birks."

"What sort of papers?"

"Divorce papers."

"Why come here?"

"I think you can tell me where he is."

"Well, I can't."

"If you could, there'd be a bit of coin in it for you."

I saw her eyes light with interest. "How much coin?"

"Perhaps quite a bit. It depends."

"What does it depend on?"

"What Mrs. Birks gets out of it."

"No, thanks. I'm not interested. I don't think that dodo can get a damn cent."

"Her divorce complaint doesn't read that way."

"It takes more than a complaint to make a divorce. It takes a judgment of a court. Mrs. Birks is one of those baby-faced bitches who hide behind a mask of respectability. She's been cheating on Morgan ever since they were married. If Morgan wanted to tell half of the things he's got on her—Oh well, you're talking, I'm listening."

"Well, Mrs. Birks can get her divorce."

"Can she?"

"You know she can," I said. "And if she wanted to be mean she could drag you into it. She's got all the evidence she needs. The way she treats you depends on the way you treat her."

"Oh, that's it, is it?" she asked, putting down the buffer and raising her eyes to mine.

"That's it," I said.

She sighed. "You looked like such a nice boy, too. How about a drink?"

"No, thanks. I don't drink when I'm working."

"You're working now?"

"Yes."

"I'm sorry about you," she said.

"You don't need to be."

"Just what does she threaten to do to me?"

"Threaten?" I asked.

"Yes."

"Why, nothing. I'm merely telling you things."

"Just as a friend, I suppose," she said sarcastically.

"Just as a friend."

"Well, just what do you want *me* to do?"

"Get Morgan Birks to acknowledge service of this summons

or else fix things so I can make a service on Birks. After all," I said, "it's to your interest to have the divorce go through, isn't it?"

"I don't know," she countered, and her face was worried. "I wish I did."

I said nothing.

"How am I supposed to fix it so you can serve the papers?"

"You make a date with Morgan Birks," I said. "Then you telephone B. L. Cool at Main 6—9321. I come over and serve the papers."

"And when do I get the pay-off?"

"You don't get any."

She threw back her head and laughed. There seemed to be genuine amusement in her laugh. "All right, sweetheart. I wanted to see what made you tick. I've found out. Get the hell out of here. Go tell Mrs. Birks she can go jump in the lake. If she wants to mention my name, ask her about her little sweetheart, Archie Holoman. Ask her if she thinks her husband is just a plain damn fool."

Her laughter followed me out into the corridor.

I went back to where Alma Hunter was waiting for me in the automobile. "See her?" she asked.

"Uh huh."

"What sort of a girl is she?" she asked curiously.

"Peroxide blonde," I said. "Easy on the eyes, and hard on the ears."

"What did she say?"

"She told me to go roll my hoop."

"Wasn't that what you wanted her to say?"

"Yes, in a way, it was."

"Why, I thought that was just what you wanted. I thought

you wanted her to get hard and kick you out and then lead you to Morgan."

"I gathered," I said, "that was the idea."

"What was it she said you didn't like?"

"There are some things about being a detective which go against the grain. I suppose a detective has to be something of a heel. At any rate, she seemed to think so."

For a long moment, Alma Hunter was silent. Then she asked, "Did she sell *you* on the idea?"

I said, "Yes," and climbed in the car to sit beside her. After a while I said, "We'd better move the car down to that alley. We can watch just as well from there, and we won't be so conspicuous."

She stretched out a neatly shod foot and pushed the starter into action. She drove the car down to the alley entrance, backed it in, found a shady place, and parked. "You're not a heel," she said. "You're nice."

"Thanks for the reassurance," I said, "but somehow it takes more than words to take the taste out of my mind."

"What did you expect the job would be like?" she asked.

"I don't know as I expected," I said.

"Weren't you attracted to it because of the idea of romance and adventure?"

"I was attracted to it because of the possibility of getting two meals a day, and a place to sleep at night. I didn't even know what kind of a job it was when I answered the ad—and I didn't much care."

She put her hand on my arm. "Don't feel bitter, Don. After all, it isn't as bad as you think. That Durke woman is the worst kind of a gold-digger. She doesn't care a fig about Morgan. She is just playing him for what she can get out of him."

"I know," I said, "but I just don't like the idea of being a heel. Not that I'm going to crab too much about it, I just didn't like it. That was all."

"But you did it?" she asked.

"I think I made a damn good job of it," I said.

She laughed then, a laugh that had a catch in it. "You say the most unexpected things, Donald. I guess it's the way you look at life. Tell me, what happened to you that leaves you so down on the world?"

"Good Lord! Do I create that sort of an impression?"

"In a way."

"I'll try to get over it."

"But tell me, Don, isn't it true?"

"I had a raw deal," I said. "When you've worked for years to get somewhere, overcome all sorts of obstacles, and get what you want, only to have someone knock it out of your hands, you have some readjusting to do."

"Was it a woman, Don?"

"No."

"Do you want to tell me about it?"

"No."

She sat looking meditatively through the windshield. Her fingers toyed with my coat sleeve.

"You were disappointed when you found I wasn't a veteran detective," I said.

"Was I?"

"Yes. Why?"

"Why, I didn't know that I was."

I turned so I could see her profile. "Was it," I asked, "because someone had been trying to choke you, and you wanted my advice on protection?"

I saw her features twist with emotion, her eyes become star-tled, her hand involuntarily go to her throat as though to shut off my gaze.

I said, "Who tried to choke you, Alma?"

The lips quivered. Tears glistened in her eyes. Her fingertips dug into my arm. I put my arm around her and drew her to me. She laid her head against my shoulder and cried, deep sobbing that spoke of tortured nerves. I slid my left hand up around her neck, put the fingertips under the chin, moved the right hand up along her blouse.

"Oh no, no," she sobbed, and grabbed at my wrist with both of her hands.

I looked down into her frightened, tear-flooded eyes. Her quivering lips were upturned—slightly parted.

There wasn't any conscious volition about kissing her. I just found my lips clinging to hers, the taste of her tears, salt on my lips. She let go of my wrist then, drew me down close to her, half turned her body with a quick twist so that she was clinging to me.

After a moment, our lips separated. I raised my right hand along her blouse, fumbled with the fastenings at the neck, part-ed it, and drew away the silk.

She was limp in my arms, making no resistance. The sobbing had quieted.

"When did this happen, Alma?" I asked.

"Last night," she said.

"How did it happen? Who was it?"

She clung to me, and I could feel her tremble.

"Poor kid," I said, and kissed her again.

We sat there in the car, our lips held together, her body close and warm against mine. The bitterness and tension flowed out of me. I ceased to hate the world. A peaceful feeling took possession of me. It wasn't passion. It wasn't that kind of a kiss. I don't know what kind of a kiss it was because I'd never had one before like it. She did things to me—things which I'd never before experienced.

Her sobbing ceased. She quit kissing me, gave a nervous, quivering little gasp, opened her purse, took out a square of handkerchief, and started drying her tears.

"I'm a sight," she said, looking in the mirror on the inside of her purse. "Has Sally Durke come out yet?"

The question brought me back to realities with a jump. I peered through the windshield of the car at the entrance of the apartment house. It was forbiddingly inanimate. A dozen Sally Durkes could have come out and gone away, and I'd have been none the wiser.

"She hasn't left, has she?" Alma asked.

"I don't know," I said. "I hope not."

There was something throaty in her laugh. "I hope not," she said. "I feel a lot better. I—I like to be kissed by you, Donald."

I wanted to say something and couldn't. It was as though I was seeing and hearing her for the first time. Little cadences in her voice, little tricks of expression were registering with me for the first time. God, I must have been bitter not to have seen her. She had been with me for hours and yet this was the first time I'd really noticed her. Now, all of my attention was concentrated on her presence. I couldn't think of anything else. I could feel the warmth of her body coming through her clothes where her legs were pressed against mine.

She seemed to have perfect control of herself, making her face over, applying lipstick with the tip of her finger.

Once more I tried to say something and couldn't. I didn't

even know what I wanted to say. It was like wanting to sing and not being able to.

I turned my attention back to the apartment house, and tried to concentrate on watching for Sally Durke. I wished I had some way of telling whether she'd gone out. I thought of going back to the apartment house and ringing her doorbell. That would let me know whether she was in, but I couldn't think of anything to say if she was in. Then, she'd know I was shadowing her—or would she? At any rate, she'd know I was hanging around.

Alma raised her hand and started to button the collar of her blouse.

"Do you," I asked, "want to tell me about that now?"

"Yes," she said, and then after a moment added, "I'm frightened, Donald. I guess I'm an awful baby."

"What are you frightened of?"

"I don't know."

"Don't you think the arrival of Sandra's brother will make a difference?"

"No. . . . That is, I shouldn't say that. I just don't know."

"What do you know about him, Alma?"

"Not very much. Whenever Sandra speaks of him, she says they didn't get along very well."

"You mean recently?"

"Well, yes."

"What does she say about him?"

"Just that he's peculiar and very independent. The fact that Sandra's his sister doesn't mean a thing to him."

"And yet she turned to him when she needed help?"

"I don't know," Alma Hunter said. "I think he came to her. That is, I think he got in touch with her by long distance telephone. I don't know. I have an idea—tell me, Donald, do you suppose there's any chance he's in partnership with Morgan?"

"What do you mean? On this slot-machine business?"

"Yes."

"There's a chance of anything," I said. "What makes you ask?"

"I don't know. Just from the way he seems to be acting, and from a remark Sandra let drop, and—while you were there in the room with him, I could hear a little of the conversation, not all of it, but a word here and there which gave me the general drift."

"Morgan is," I said, "a husband. He's a defendant in a divorce action. The papers are going to be served on him. Then he'll either come into court, or he'll default and cease being a husband. Therefore, why worry about it?"

"Because I think you can't dispose of him as simply as that. I think he's—dangerous."

"Now," I said, "we're getting to the point I wanted to talk about."

"What?"

"Those bruises on your neck."

"Oh, he has nothing to do with them."

"Go ahead. Tell me about it. Who was it?"

"A b-b-burglar."

"Where?"

"Someone who broke into the apartment."

"When?"

"Last night."

"You two girls were there alone?"

"Yes."

"Where was Sandra?"

"She slept in the other bedroom."

"And you were sleeping in the room with the twin beds?"

"Yes."

"Sandra was sleeping in the room where Bleatie is now?"

"Yes."

"And what happened?"

"I don't know," she said. "—Oh, I shouldn't tell you about it. I promised Sandra I wouldn't say anything to anyone."

"Why all the secrecy?"

"Because she's having enough trouble with the police. They're trying to locate Morgan, and they've been coming in at all hours of the day and night and asking all sorts of questions. It's been very embarrassing."

"So I imagine, but that's no reason why you should be choked to death."

"I fought him off."

"How did it happen?"

"It was a hot night," she said. "I was sleeping without very much on. I woke up and a man was leaning over the bed. I moved and started to scream. He grabbed me by the throat and I began to kick. I kicked him in the stomach with my heels and got my knees up against his shoulders and pushed with all of my might. If I'd slept just a second longer, and he'd got closer to me, he'd have choked me; but when I got my knees up and pushed, I finally broke his hold."

"And then what happened?"

"And then he ran."

"Where?"

"Out into the other room."

"And then what?"

"Then I called Sandra. We turned on the lights, and looked through the apartment. Nothing was disturbed."

"Did you find how he got in?"

"It must have been by the fire escape because the door was locked."

"Was he dressed?" I asked.

"I don't know. I didn't see him. It was dark."

"But you could feel, couldn't you?"

"Well, yes, in a way."

"And you never did see him? You wouldn't recognize him if you saw him again?"

"No, it was dark as pitch."

"Look here, Alma," I said. "You're nervous. There's more to this than you're telling me. Why don't you give me a chance to help you?"

"No," she said, "I can't—I mean, there isn't—I've told you everything."

I sat back and smoked a cigarette in silence. After a minute, she said, "You're really truly a detective, aren't you? I mean legally?"

"Yes."

"And you have a right to carry a gun?"

"I suppose so."

"Could you—could you get a gun if I gave you the money, and let me carry it for a while?"

"Why?"

"Protection."

"Why the gun?"

"Why not?" she asked. "Good Lord, if you'd wakened in the middle of the night and found someone leaning over you, and then hands clutching at your throat and—"

"Then you think it's going to happen again?"

"I don't know, but I want to stay with Sandra, and I think she's in danger."

"What's she in danger of?"

"I don't know. I think someone's trying to kill her."

"Why her?"

"You see, I was sleeping in her bed."

"Her husband perhaps?"

"No, I don't think it's her husband, but—well, it might have been."

"Leave her," I said. "Go get a room by yourself and—"

"No, I couldn't do that. I'm her friend. I'm going to stand by her. She's stood by me."

"Has she?"

"Yes."

"I gathered from her brother she was rather selfish, a woman who—"

"Well, she isn't," she interrupted. "What does her brother know about her? My God, he's never paid the faintest attention to her. I don't think he's written to her once in five years."

"He seemed to know a lot about her."

"That's what makes me think he's standing in with Morgan. I think Morgan put those ideas in his head. Morgan's been talking about her, saying the most horrible things, that she's sex-crazy and has a new man on the string all the time, and all that sort of stuff, things that no man should say about a woman, least of all about his wife."

"I gather their domestic life hasn't been particularly happy?"

"Of course it hasn't. But that's no reason a man should go around making a lot of false statements about the woman he's sworn to love and protect—sometimes men make me sick."

"Let's go back to the reason for your interest in Mrs. Cool's marital venture."

"What do you mean by that?"

"I thought you took an unusual interest in it."

"It was interesting."

"Doubly interesting to one who is contemplating marriage."

"Or running away from marriage," she said, smiling up at me.

"Is that what you're doing?"

She nodded.

"Want to tell me about it?"

She hesitated a moment, then said, "No, Donald, I'd rather not—not right now, anyway."

"From Kansas City?" I asked.

"Yes. One of those crazy, insanely jealous men who are always looking for an excuse to get drunk and smash things."

"Don't waste time on him," I said. "I know the breed. They're all the same. They have a fierce, possessive desire to own a woman, body and soul. He probably tried to tell you that his jealousy is only because he really doesn't have the legal right to love and cherish you the way he wants, that if you were only his wife, he wouldn't mind, that if you'd marry him, things would all be hunky-dory; and whenever you refuse, he goes out and gets drunk. He comes back and makes a scene, smashes glassware, and—"

"You sound as though you knew him," she interrupted.

"I do, not as an individual, but as a type."

"And your advice is to lay off?"

"Absolutely. Any time a man can't show his strength of character by beating down his own faults, and then tries to get his self-respect back by smashing a dish, you want to lay off of him."

"His particular yen is smashing glasses in a bar," she said.

"You're not going to marry him?"

"No."

"He's in Kansas City?"

"Yes—that is, he was when I left. If he knew where I was, he'd follow."

"And then what?"

"I don't know, smash some dishes perhaps."

"Those men are poison," I said. "They'll pay any price for the opportunity to assert themselves."

"I know," she said. "You read about them every day in the papers, the men who track down estranged wives, shoot them, and then commit suicide—the final gesture of futility—I hate it, and I'm afraid of it."

I looked at her sharply. "And is it because of that you want the gun?"

She met my eyes then, and said, "Yes."

"Do you want to buy one?"

"Yes, of course."

"You have the money?"

"Yes."

"It's going to take about twenty-five dollars," I said.

She opened her purse, took out two tens and a five, and gave them to me.

"I can't get it right now," I told her, "because we're going to have to watch for that Durke girl to come out. I wonder why Bleatie was so positive she'd go somewhere to get in touch with Morgan Birks. You'd think she'd use the telephone."

"Probably her line's tapped," Alma said.

"No, the police don't know anything about her. If they did, they'd shadow her."

"Well, she probably thinks the telephone's tapped, or perhaps Morgan thinks so."

"It doesn't make sense," I said, "but then in real life things seldom do make—There she comes!"

Sally Durke walked out of the apartment house with an overnight bag in her hand. She was tailored up to the minute in a blue skirt and jacket. The skirt was cut short, and her ankles were enough to make any man turn around. She wore a close-fitting blue hat tilted at an angle with a rakish little bow of blue velvet. Her flaxen hair, peeking out from under the hat, showed up soft and golden against the blue.

"What makes you think she's peroxide?" Alma Hunter asked, as she started the motor.

"I don't know. Something about the color of her hair. It's—"

"She looks like a natural blonde from here—looks pretty."

"Far be it from me to argue about feminine beauty with an expert," I said. "Careful not to crowd too close. She's headed for the boulevard. Let her get enough of a lead so she won't look back and see us crawling along. That'll make her suspicious."

"I thought I'd run out into the street and then stop until we can see what she does."

"Okay, good girl. Want me to drive?"

"If you wouldn't mind, I'd like it a lot. I'm nervous."

I said, "All right. Come out from behind the wheel, and I'll slide under."

She moved over from behind the wheel, raised herself, and I slid under. I slipped the gears into mesh, then kicked out the clutch, and let the machine inch along close to the curb.

Sally Durke walked to the corner and flagged a passing taxicab. I speeded the car and made the turn into the boulevard not over fifty feet behind the cab. Then I gradually dropped behind, waiting to see if she looked back.

She didn't. Her head showed through the rear window in the cab, her eyes apparently fixed straight ahead.

"Looks like a cinch," I said, and closed the distance between the car and the cab.

The cab rolled smoothly along, made no attempt to shake off pursuit, turned to the left when it got to Sixteenth Street and went to the Perkins Hotel. There wasn't any parking place in sight. I said to Alma, "This is where you have to pinch-hit. Get in behind the wheel and keep driving around the block. I want to get in there right after she registers and see what room she gets. I'll give her time enough to get out of the lobby and that's all."

Alma Hunter said, "Look here. I want to be in on this thing."

"You're in on it," I said.

"No, not that way. I want to be in at the finish. What are you going to do?"

"Find out what room she has, and get a room directly across from it if possible."

"I want to stay with you."

"No chance," I said. "Sorry, but that's out. The better-class hotels get snooty when a man starts entertaining women in his room. The bellboys try to work a little blackmail, and—"

"Oh shucks," she said, "don't be like that! Go register as man and wife. What name are you going to use?"

"Donald Helforth."

"All right, I'll be Mrs. Helforth. I'll come in later and join you. Get started."

I went across to the hotel. Sally Durke wasn't in sight. I told a bellboy to get me the bell captain, and took the captain off into executive session. "A blonde in a blue outfit came in about two minutes ago," I said. "I want to know what name she registered under, where she's registered, and what rooms near her are vacant. I'd like to get one across the corridor from her if I can."

"What's the idea?" he asked.

I took a five-dollar bill from my pocket, folded it, twisted it around my fingers, and said, "I'm a committee of one, working on behalf of the government, trying to get deserving bellboys into the higher income brackets so we can collect more tax."

"I always co-operate with the government," he said, grinning. "Just a minute."

I waited in the lobby until he came back with the information. She was Mrs. B. F. Morgan and was in 618. She expected her husband to join her shortly. The only vacant room anywhere in that part of the hotel was 620, and Mrs. Morgan, it seemed, had reserved 618 earlier in the day by telephone, said she might want 620 as well, and had asked the management to hold that. When she registered, she said she'd changed her mind about 620 and would only want 618.

"I'm Donald Helforth," I said. "My wife, about twenty-five, with chestnut hair and brown eyes, will be coming in within five or ten minutes. Keep an eye out for her, and show her up to my room, will you?"

"Your wife?" he asked.

"My wife," I said.

"Oh, I see."

"And here's one other thing. I want a gun."

His eyes lost their friendliness. "What sort of a gun?"

"A small gun that fits in the pocket nicely, preferably an automatic. And I want a box of shells for it."

"You're supposed to have a police permit in order to get a gun," he said.

"And when you have a police permit, you buy your gun at a store and pay about fifteen dollars for it," I said. "What the hell do you think I'm paying twenty-five bucks for a gun for?"

"Oh, you're paying twenty-five bucks for it?"

"That's what I said."

"I'll see what I can do."

I didn't give him any chance to tip off the room clerk, but walked directly to the desk. The clerk handed me a card, and I wrote, "Donald Helforth and wife," and gave a fictitious address.

"Something at about seven dollars a day, Mr. Helforth?" the clerk asked.

"What do you have on the sixth floor? I don't want to be too high, and yet I want to be far enough above the traffic to keep the street cars out of my ears."

He looked at the chart and said, "I could give you 675."

"Which end of the house is that?"

"The east."

"What do you have on the west?"

"I could give you 605, or I can give you 620."

"What about 620?"

"Twin beds and a bath. The rates are seven and a half double."

"Can't you make it seven?" I asked.

He looked me over, and said he'd make a special concession.

"All right," I said. "My wife will be in later with my baggage, but I'll pay for the room now."

I gave him the money, took a receipt, and went up to my room with the bell captain. "You can't get a new gun for twenty-five bucks," he objected.

"Who said anything about a new gun? You're getting one

from a second-hand store somewhere. Twenty-five is my limit, and don't try to chisel too much profit. Get one that costs at least fifteen."

"I'd be breaking the law," he said.

"No, you wouldn't."

"Why not?"

I took from my pocket the authorization Mrs. Cool had signed for me. "I'm a private detective," I said.

He looked it over, and the perplexity left his face. "All right, boss. I'll see what I can do."

"Make it snappy," I told him, "but don't go out until my wife comes in. I want her to be taken right up here."

"Right," he said, and went out.

I looked around the room. It was an ordinary twin-bed affair in an ordinary hotel. I went into the bathroom. It was designed so that 618 and 620 could be opened up together as adjoining rooms with the bath in between. I tried the knob on the connecting door slowly and carefully. The door was locked. Listening, I could hear the sounds of someone moving around in the adjoining room. I went back to the telephone and called Sandra Birks. When I had her on the line, I said, "Everything seems to be okay. I've followed her to the Perkins Hotel. She's in 618, registered under the name of Morgan, and has left word at the desk her husband is joining her. Alma and I are here at the hotel as Mr. and Mrs. Donald Helforth in 620."

"*Mr. and Mrs?*" Sandra Birks asked with rising inflection.

"Yes. Alma wanted to be in on it."

"In on what?"

"On the service of the papers," I said.

"Well, I want to be in on it, too. I hate to interrupt your honeymoon, but Bleatie and I are coming up."

"Now, look here," I objected, "if Morgan Birks should happen to be hanging around the hotel and sees you drive up, it'll just be too bad. We'll never get a chance to serve him again."

"I understand that," she said. "I'll be careful."

"You can't be careful. You can't tell whether you'll run into him in the lobby, in the elevator, or in the corridor. He may be watching the place now for all you know. He—"

"You shouldn't have let Alma share the room with you," Sandra Birks said in a dignified voice. "After all, you know, Mr. Lam, this thing may come up in court."

"Bosh. I'm simply serving papers," I said.

"I'm afraid," she cooed, "you don't understand. Alma simply can't afford to have her name in the papers. Bleatie and I will be right up. Good-by." And the telephone clicked.

I hung up the receiver, took off my coat, washed my face and hands, sat down in the chair, and lit a cigarette. Someone knocked on the door. Before I could get up, the bellboy opened it and said, "Here you are, Mrs. Helforth."

Alma came in, saying, in a voice she tried to keep casual, "Hello, dear. I thought I'd better park the car before I came in. They're going to deliver some packages for me later on."

I walked over to the bellboy whose expression showed that Alma's amateurish attempt at domestic deception was giving him a quiet laugh. "Some other people are coming in," I said. "They'll probably be here within ten or fifteen minutes. I want that gun before they get here."

"I'll have to have some money. I—"

I gave him the two tens and a five. "Make it snappy," I said, "and don't forget the shells. Have it done up in brown paper. Don't give the package to anyone but me. Get started."

"On my way," he said, and shot out of the door.

"What gun are you talking about, the one you were getting for me?" Alma asked.

"Yes," I said. "Sandra and Bleatie are coming up here. Your friend Sandra seems to think I've irrevocably ruined your good name in letting you in on this. She refers to it as 'sharing my room.'"

Alma laughed. "Good old Sandra," she said, "is so scrupulously careful about protecting *my* good name, yet she—"

"And yet she does what?" I asked as her voice faded out like a distant radio station.

"Nothing," she said.

"Come on, let's have it."

"No, nothing. Honestly, I wasn't going to say anything."

"Much," I said. "I'd like to know what Sandra does."

"It isn't important."

"Anyway, she's coming up here. Before she arrives, I want to take a look at your neck."

"At my neck?"

"Yes, at those bruises. I want to see something."

I stepped forward and slid my left arm around the back of her shoulder, fumbled with the silken loop which circled some ornamental buttons on the collar of her blouse.

"No, no," she said. "Don't. Please—" She raised her hand to push me away, but I slipped the loop over the button and opened her blouse. Her head came back. Her lips were close to mine. Her arm slid over my shoulders, and I pulled her to me. Her lips were warm and clinging. This time there was no taste of salt tears. After a while, she drew away and said, "Oh, Donald, what *must* you think of me?"

"I think you're swell," I said.

"Donald, I don't usually do this. I have been feeling so lonesome and all alone—and from the first time I met you—"

I kissed her again. After that, I gently slid the blouse away from her neck and looked at the bruised marks. She stood perfectly still. I could feel her even, regular breathing, but a pulse in her neck was throbbing rapidly.

"How big was this man who tried to choke you?" I asked.

"I don't know. I tell you it was dark."

"Was he big and fat, or small and thin?"

"He wasn't fat."

"His hands must have been small."

"Well—I don't know—"

"Look here," I said, "there are little scratches on the skin which could have been made by fingernails. Now, are you certain it wasn't a woman?"

She caught her breath at that. "Scratches?" she asked.

"Yes, scratches, nail scratches. The person who choked you must have had long, pointed fingernails. Now why couldn't it have been a woman as well as a man?"

"Because I don't think—no, I think it was a man."

"But you couldn't see anything at all?"

"No."

"It was pitch dark?"

"Yes."

"And whoever it was made no sound?"

"No."

"Simply started to choke you and you fought free?"

"Yes, I pushed him away."

"And you have absolutely no idea who it was?" I asked.

"No."

"There's nothing whatever to give you a clue?"

"No."

I patted her shoulder. "All right, dear. I just wanted to find out. That's all."

"I—I think I'll sit down," she said. "I get nervous every time I talk about it."

She went over to the overstuffed chair and sat down.

"I think you'd better tell me about your boy friend," I said.

"He's in Kansas City."

"But you don't think he's going to stay there?"

"If he finds out where I am, he may come here."

"Don't you think he's found out already?"

"No. He couldn't have found out."

"And yet in the back of your mind there's the thought that he may have—"

"Don't, Donald, please," she interrupted. "I don't think I can take any more."

"All right," I said. "You don't have to. Better button up your blouse. Sandra and Bleatie may be here any minute."

She raised her hands to her blouse. I saw the fingers quiver as she fitted the loops over the buttons.

Afternoon sun streamed into the room, made it hot and close. There was no breeze, and the open windows seemed merely to attract the hot air which radiated up from the side of the building.

The bell captain knocked at the door, pushed a brown paper package into my hands. "Listen, buddy," he said, "don't get into any trouble with this rod. It's a good one, but I had to lie like hell to get old Mose to let loose of it."

I said, "Thanks," kicked the door shut, ripped off the brown wrappings, and brought to light a thirty-two blue-steel automatic. The blue was worn off the steel in places; but the barrel was in good condition. I opened the box of shells, pushed the magazine full, and said to Alma Hunter, "You know how to work this?"

"No," she said.

"Here's a safety catch that you work with your thumb," I explained. "Here's another safety catch on the back of the handle which you automatically release when you squeeze your hand about the grip. All you have to do is to hold it in your right hand, pull this little lever down with your thumb, and pull the trigger. Do you understand?"

"I think so."

"Let's see if you do." I removed the magazine, jerked the mechanism back and forth, snapped the safety catch into position, handed it to her, and said, "Shoot me."

She took the gun and said, "Donald, don't say that."

"Point it at me," I said. "Shoot me. You've got to. I'm going to choke you. Come on, Alma, snap out of it. Let's see if you can point the gun and pull the trigger."

She pointed the gun and tried to pull the trigger. The skin grew white across her knuckles, but nothing happened.

"The safety catch," I said.

She jerked the catch down with her thumb. I heard the click of the firing pin against the chamber, and then she sat down on the bed as though her knees had lost all their strength. The gun dropped from her limp fingers to the carpet.

I picked up the gun, shoved the magazine back into position, jacked a shell up into the chamber, saw that the safety catch was on, removed the magazine, and shoved in a shell to take the place of the one that had gone up into the firing chamber. I put the gun in her purse.

She watched me with frightened, fascinated eyes.

I wrapped the extra box of shells in the brown paper and dropped it into the bureau drawer. Then I went over and sat down on the bed beside her. "Listen, Alma," I said, "that gun's loaded. Don't shoot anyone unless you *have to,* but if anyone starts playing with your neck again, you start making noises with that gun. You don't need to hit him. Just cut loose with the gun. That will bring help."

She stretched out on the bed, and twisted her lithe, supple body around to mine with a gesture that reminded me of a kitten twisting around in play. Her arms came around my neck, drew me to her. I felt the tip of her tongue searching my lips.

It was perhaps an hour later that a quick succession of knocks announced the arrival of Sandra Birks and her brother.

I opened the door.

"Where's Alma?" Sandra Birks asked.

"In the bathroom," I said, "washing her eyes. She's nervous and upset. She's been crying."

"And I presume," Sandra said, looking at the rumpled bed, "you were comforting her."

Bleatie stared down at the pillow and said, "Hell, they're all the same."

Sandra turned on him. "You shut up, Bleatie," she said. "You have a dirty mind. You don't think any woman's decent."

"Well," he said, "what were *you* thinking?"

I said, "Did you see anything of Morgan Birks?"

Sandra seemed anxious to change the subject. "No, we came in the back way, bribed the porter to take us up in the freight elevator."

Alma came out of the bathroom.

"*She* hasn't been crying," Bleatie said.

Sandra ignored him. "What's going on in the next room?" she asked.

"Miss Sally Durke has become Mrs. B. F. Morgan," I said. "She's waiting for Mr. Morgan to join her. Doubtless it'll be before dinner. They may have dinner served in their room."

"We can prop this door open and listen," Sandra Birks said.

"You don't give your husband credit for very much intelligence, do you?" I asked.

"Why?"

"He'd spot that open door before he was halfway down the corridor. No, we'll have to take turns listening at the bathroom door. We can hear him when he comes in."

Bleatie said, "I've got a scheme that beats that all to pieces." He took a pocket drill from his pocket, tiptoed into the bathroom, listened a minute, and said, "The place to bore holes in a door is right in the corner of the panel."

"Put that thing away," I said. "You'll just spill wood particles all over the floor and put her wise."

"Have you any plans?" he asked me.

"Plenty of them. We take turns listening at the bathroom. When we hear a man come in, I go around to their room. If it's Morgan Birks, I serve the papers on him."

"You'll recognize him from his photographs?" Sandra Birks asked.

"Yes, I've studied them carefully."

"How are you going to get in?" Bleatie asked me.

"I'm going to ring the room, tell them it's the office talking, that there's a telegram for Mr. B. F. Morgan, and ask if I shall send it up."

"That's an old dodge. They'll get suspicious, and tell you to slip it under the door."

"Don't worry. I'll have the telegram and a registration book. I won't be able to get the book under the door. I'll try. The telegram will be real."

"They'll open the door a crack, see you, and slam it shut."

"Not when they see me, they won't," I said. "I'm going out and collect the stage properties. You stay here and hold the fort. Don't get excited if Morgan comes in. I'll be back inside of half an hour. He's certain to stay at least that long. Remember, she's brought an overnight bag."

"I don't like it," Bleatie said. "It sounds crude and—"

"Everything sounds crude when you outline it in cold conversation," I said. "It's the build-up. Look at all the bunco games which are pulled by the slickers. You read about them in the newspapers, and they seem so crude you can't imagine anyone falling for them. Yet people fall for them three hundred and sixty-five days out of the year just like clockwork. It's the build-up."

"Nevertheless, I still think it's crude. I—"

I didn't see any sense debating it with him. I slipped out of the door and into the corridor, leaving him to explain to the others how crude it was.

CHAPTER SIX

I WAS gone about an hour. When I came back, I had a bellboy's uniform which I'd rented from a costume house, a telegram I'd sent myself, under the name of B. F. Morgan, and a notebook with ruled pages, half a dozen of which had been scrawled with signatures that I'd faked with lead pencil and fountain pen.

I tapped gently on the door of my room in the hotel.

Alma Hunter opened it.

Looking past the open door, I saw Bertha Cool squeezed into the big, overstuffed chair, filling it to overflowing. A bottle of Scotch, some ice, and a siphon of soda were on the table beside her. She was sipping from a tall glass. Sandra Birks came gliding toward me, like some supple shadow. "Oh you bungler!" she said. "You've ruined things."

"Why the bouquets?" I asked, my eye drifting past her to rest apprehensively on the head of the Cool Detective Agency.

"For God's sake, close the door," Bertha Cool said to Sandra. "If you want to bellyache, go ahead and do it, but don't advertise your troubles to the hotel. Come on in, Donald."

I walked in and Alma Hunter closed the door. I couldn't see Bleatie anywhere. The bathroom door was closed. I could hear voices coming from behind the door.

"What's the trouble?" I asked.

"You went away and didn't tell anyone where you were going," Sandra Birks said. "You had that original summons and the copy for service, and Morgan has been in there for an hour. He came in just a few minutes after you left. Of all the dumb, bonehead tricks—"

"Where is he now?" I asked.

"He's still there,—I hope."

"Where's your brother?"

"He had a hemorrhage. His broken nose started to bleed back into his mouth, and I telephoned for the doctor. It may be serious. He and the doctor are in the bathroom."

Bertha Cool said, "You evidently started something, Donald. Mrs. Birks telephoned me to try and find where you were. Why don't you keep in touch with the office?"

"Because you told me you didn't want reports. You wanted the papers served," I said. "If I'm let alone long enough, I'll serve them. I'm sorry you were disturbed. It's what I get for trying to be polite and letting Mrs. Birks know what is going on. I wasn't in favor of her and her brother coming up here in the first place."

"That's all nonsense," Sandra Birks said coldly. "You're trying to dodge responsibility by putting the blame on us."

"I'm not putting the blame on anyone," I said. "If your brother's having a hemorrhage in the bathroom, I'm going to change into this bellboy suit in the closet. I suggest you try keeping your back turned."

Sandra Birks said, "The papers. We want those papers. My God, we've been telephoning frantically—"

"Keep your shirt on," I said. "I'm supposed to serve these papers, and I'm going to. Do you know that it's Morgan in there?"

"Yes, you can hear his voice through the bathroom door."

I glanced across at Bertha Cool. "How long have you been here?" I asked.

"About ten minutes," she said. "My God, you'd have thought the place was on fire, the way they've been burning up the wire. If Morgan Birks gets away from you, Donald, I'm going to be very angry about it."

I didn't say anything. I went in the closet, unwrapped the costume, got out of my clothes, and put on my bellboy's uniform. There was no light in the closet so I left the door ajar to see to make the change. Through the open door, I could hear what was taking place in the other room. I heard Alma Hunter say, "I think you're unjust, Sandra. He had to use his best judgment, didn't he?"

Sandra said, "His best judgment wasn't good enough, that's all," and then I heard the glug-glug-glug-glug of whisky being poured from a bottle which was almost full, the hiss of siphon water and Bertha Cool's calm voice saying, "After all, Mrs. Birks, he let you in on this. If he hadn't telephoned you, you wouldn't have known a damn thing about it. We're hired to serve papers. If Morgan Birks has left and Donald can't serve the papers, then it's a horse on me. If Morgan Birks is still there and Donald serves the papers, you're going to be charged for getting me to drop everything else and come rushing out here as fast as a cab could bring me."

Sandra Birks said, "Well, if you want to know the truth, I think my attorney made a mistake in recommending you. I'm sorry that I ever came to your agency."

"Yes," Mrs. Cool said in the voice of a perfect lady discussing the latest novel, "it *is* regrettable, isn't it, dearie?"

I came out of the closet, buttoning up the bellboy's coat around my neck. I took the yellow envelope with the telegram and the notebook, walked over to the telephone, and said to the operator, "Ring 618, please." A moment later, when I heard a woman's voice on the line, I said, "There's a telegram for Mrs. B. F. Morgan."

"I'm not expecting any telegram," she said. "No one knows I'm here."

"Yes, Mrs. Morgan. This telegram has a very peculiar address. It reads: 'Mrs. B. F. Morgan, Perkins Hotel, or deliver to Sally Durke.' Now, we have no Durke registered here."

"Well, I'm certain I don't know what it's about," she said, but her voice was a little less positive than it had been.

"I'll send it up," I said, "and you can look at it. Open it if you want to and see if the message is for you—you have a right to do that, you know. Boy, oh boy! Telegram to 618." I hung up.

Bertha Cool dropped more ice into her glass, and said, "Better make it snappy, Donald, she'll call the office to verify the information."

I tucked the book under my arm, unlocked the door, and stepped out into the corridor. The three of them stood looking after me. I walked down to 618 and tapped on the door.

I could hear a woman's voice talking over the telephone, and said, "Telegram."

The woman's voice quit talking. Then I heard her on the other side of the door.

"Slide it under the door," she said.

I squeezed the notebook partially under the door, so that she could see just the edge of the yellow envelope in between the leaves. "I can't make it," I said. "You have to sign for it. The book won't go under the door."

She said, "Just a minute, I'll unlock the door."

She unlocked the door and opened it a crack, stood staring

out at me suspiciously. I kept my face lowered. When she saw my uniform and the telegram in the book, she opened the door six or eight inches. "Where do I sign?" she asked.

"Right on this line," I told her, shoving the book through the door and handing her a pencil.

She was wearing a rose-colored robe over not very much of anything. I looked through the crack in the open door and could see nothing, so I pushed the door open and walked in.

At first she didn't get the idea. Then as the light fell on my face, she recognized me. "Morgan!" she cried. "Look out! It's a detective."

Morgan Birks, attired in a double-breasted gray suit, was lying on the bed, his ankles crossed, a cigarette in his mouth. I walked over to him and said, "This is an original summons, Mr. Birks, in the case of Sandra Birks versus Morgan Birks. This is a copy of the summons and a copy of the complaint which I hand you herewith."

He calmly removed the cigarette from his lips, blew smoke at the ceiling, and said, "Pretty smart, aren't you, buddy?"

Sally Durke came running up behind me, her rose-colored robe trailing out behind her. She had ripped the yellow envelope open and pulled out the fake message. She slammed the book on the floor, tore the telegram in two and flung it at me. "You damn double-crossing stool pigeon," she said.

"What else?" Birks asked me.

"That's all."

"No warrant of arrest?"

"No, this is just a civil case."

"Okay, buddy. I wish you luck."

"Thanks," I said, "and you might call off your dog. I don't like her bark."

I turned and started toward the door just as it banged open and Sandra Birks came rushing into the room. Behind her came Alma Hunter, apparently trying to pull her back. And looming behind them, a cigarette in her lips, was the huge form of Bertha Cool.

On the bed, Birks said, "Well, well, well!"

Sandra Birks shouted at him, "You dirty chiseler. So *this* is the way you've been carrying on, is it? *This* is the little hussy you've been squandering your money on. This is the way you treat your marriage vows."

Birks took the cigarette out of his mouth, yawned and said, "Yes, dearest, this is Sally Durke. I'm sorry you don't like her. Why didn't you bring your doctor friend along if you wanted to make the party complete?"

Sandra Birks sputtered indignantly. "You—you—you—"

Birks raised himself to one elbow. I could see the sharp features, the long, slender body, the tapering fingers of his hands. Light glinted from rich black hair which was combed straight back from a high forehead. "Never mind the fireworks, Sandra. You want a divorce, and you don't want it any worse than I do. Get the hell out of here."

Sandra Birks said to Bertha Cool, "I just want you to see the kind of husband I have. Look what he's doing. Carrying on up here with a dirty, faded blonde, wandering around without any clothes on."

She made a grab at the rose-colored robe. Sally Durke clutched it around her. Sandra pulled it up high enough to show bare legs and thighs. Sally Durke kicked at her face and called her a name.

Bertha Cool scooped an arm around Sandra Birks' waist and pulled her away from the fighting blonde.

"Thanks," Morgan Birks said, still sprawled on the bed. "It saves me from popping her one. For God's sake, Sandra, take a tumble to yourself. You've been two-timing me right under my nose."

"That's a lie," she said, struggling against Bertha Cool's big arm.

Alma Hunter ran to Sandra's side. "Come, Sandra," she said, "don't argue with him. The papers have been served."

Morgan Birks leaned over the side of the bed, found the cuspidor, dropped the end of his cigarette in it, and said to Sally Durke, "I'm sorry my wife is such a bitch, dearest, but she can't help it."

"If you ask me," Sally Durke said, "she needs a good beating."

I said to Bertha Cool, "I've served the papers. I'm ready to make the affidavit. That's all I have to bother about," and walked out into the corridor.

A moment later, Bertha Cool pushed Sandra Birks out ahead of her into the corridor. She was mumbling soothing words. Behind us, the door slammed and the bolt turned. We walked down to 620 and went in. I said, "I didn't know there was to be a show."

"I just couldn't help it. I wanted to confront him with the proof of his infidelity," Sandra Birks said.

The door from the bathroom opened, and Dr. Holoman came into the room. His sleeves were rolled up, his coat was off, and his shirt was spattered with water and bloodstains.

"What was all the racket about?" he asked. "And did I hear something about a doctor?"

"I'll say you did," Bertha Cool said. "And I don't think Mrs. Birks' lawyer would care very much about you being here."

"He had to come on account of Bleatie," Sandra Birks said. "How is he, Archie?"

"He's going to be all right," Dr. Holoman said, "but it's been touch-and-go. I had the devil of a time stopping that hemorrhage. He got too excited. I'm going to insist that he keep absolutely quiet for at least three days." He popped back into the bathroom and closed the door.

Sandra Birks said, "He's a beast. He's always made those rotten insinuations. I've been absolutely true to him. I've never so much as looked at another man all the time I've been married. He's even poisoned my own brother's mind against me."

I went back in the closet, changed my clothes, and wrapped up the bellboy costume.

She walked over to the door and called out, in a loud voice, "Oh, Bleatie, it's all right. He's been served."

I heard Bleatie's voice from the other side of the bathroom door saying, "Shud up. He cad hear." Then from the other room, sounding distant and mumbled, but still taunting, came Morgan Birks' voice, distinctly audible: "Bleatie, eh? So I have *you* to thank for this? I should have known it."

Bleatie sputtered into noise. "You're crazy, Morgan," he yelled in his hay-fever voice. "I stuck up for you. I've got something in my pocket to give you. Open the door." There was silence for a minute or two, then the bathroom door burst open, and Bleatie came storming into the room. He was a mess, with red stains all over his shirt and coat. "You fool!" he cried at Sandra, his voice coming thickly past the bandaged nose. "Haven't you any more sense than to yell at me like that? Didn't you know he could hear?"

"I'm sorry, Bleatie."

"Sorry, hell!" he shouted. "You never did anything in your

life you were sorry for, unless it was something that inconvenienced you. Now that the papers have been served, you don't give a damn about me. Well, I'll make it a point to see that you don't stick Morgan for a lot of alimony."

He dashed past us, jerked the door to the corridor open and ran around to room 618. He hammered on the door. Then, when there was no answer, said, pleadingly, "Morgan, let me in. It's Bleatie. I want to talk with you. I have something to tell you."

Bertha Cool finished the last of her drink and smiled benignly at the tense group in the room. After a moment, Sandra Birks moved out into the corridor where she could watch Bleatie standing in front of the door, pleading and knocking.

Bertha Cool said calmly, "Come on, Donald. We're going back to the office."

I looked over at Alma Hunter, and her glance showed me that she understood.

"I *did* have a dinner date," I said. "Something to talk over—"

Bertha Cool interrupted with calm finality. "You're going to dinner with me, Donald. We have a case to talk over. You're working for me. If Alma Hunter wants to hire my agency for any more work, I'll be glad to accept the employment and assign you to the case. This business is finished. Come on."

I took a card from my pocket, scribbled the telephone number of the boarding house where I was staying, and handed it to Alma Hunter.

"She's the boss," I said. "If you need me, you can ring me there."

Bertha Cool said to Sandra Birks, "This Scotch and soda are part of the expenses. I'll leave word at the desk that you'll settle up. Come on, Donald."

Dr. Holoman ran out into the corridor just ahead of us. He

tugged gently at Bleatie's sleeve and said in a low voice, "You'll start that hemorrhage again. Come back here."

Bleatie shook him off, pounded on the door. "Open up, Morgan, you fool," he said. "I have something that's going to help you win your case. I've been protecting you all the way through."

Dr. Holoman turned quickly away. Mrs. Cool, marching toward the elevator, almost ran him down.

He grabbed her arm desperately and said, "Look here, you can do something with him. He'll bring on a hemorrhage. Won't you try getting him back into the room?"

Mrs. Cool said "No" to him, and then to me, "Come on, Donald," and led the way down the corridor.

When we were on the sidewalk, I said, "Is this new case something I'm supposed to start on tonight?"

"What case?"

"The one you wanted to discuss at dinner."

"Oh," she said, "there isn't any case, and there won't be any dinner."

When she saw the expression on my face, she went on, "I saw you were falling for that Hunter girl. I don't like it. She's mixed in a case. We've worked on that case. Our job's finished. Forget her. And, by the way, Donald, you might signal a cab for me. Get it over here by the fireplug where he can pull into the curb, because I'm not built to go out into traffic and climb aboard a cab."

I walked out to the curb with her and signaled a cruising cab. He took a look at Bertha Cool's build and didn't like the idea of trying to load her, away from the curb, any more than she did. He switched on his lights, pulled in next to the fireplug. I assisted her in, and raised my hat.

"But you're coming, Donald," she said.

"No, I've got other places to go."

"Where?"

"Back to ask Alma Hunter for a dinner date," I said.

Her eyes locked with mine. "I'm afraid," she said, "you don't take kindly to suggestion, Donald." And her voice was the voice of an indulgent mother, censoring a child for a minor misdemeanor.

"I don't," I said.

She settled back against the cushions. "Pull down that jump seat, Donald," she said, "so I can put my feet on it, and don't be so God damn serious about it. Good night."

I raised my hat a good ten inches from my head as the taxi-cab whisked her out into traffic. Then I turned back toward the hotel and bumped into a man who was standing just behind me.

"Sorry," I said.

"What's the hurry?" he asked.

"Nothing you'd understand," I said, and tried to push past him. Another man who had been standing a step behind the first one came up to block my progress. "Take it easy, Pint-Size," he said.

"Say, what *is* this?" I asked.

"The chief wants to see you," one of the men said.

"Well, the chief has nothing on me."

The first man was tall and slender with a hawk nose and hard eyes. The other had big shoulders, slim hips, and a bull neck. His nose looked as though it had been pushed all over his face, and his right ear had a tendency to cauliflower. He had the gift of gab, and evidently liked to hear his own voice.

"Well, well, well," he said. "Our friend is pulling the old crook stall. The chief has nothing on me—how about it, buddy?

Want to talk with the chief, or shall we tell the chief that you don't care about co-operating?"

"Co-operating with what?" I asked.

"Answering questions."

"About what?"

"About Morgan Birks."

I glanced from one to the other, unostentatiously shifted my position so that I could look over toward the hotel. At any minute now Sandra Birks and her brother might come out. They'd figure I'd led them into a trap or had sold them out. I grinned up into the hard eyes of the tall man, and said, "Sure I'll come."

"That's better. We thought you would," the bruiser said, and looked anxiously down the street. A big sedan slid out of the stream of traffic, and the men pushed me across to it, one at each arm. They opened the door and popped me in, climbed in beside me, and the tall man said to the driver, "Okay, John. Let's go."

We went, but it wasn't until the car reached the residential section that I began to be suspicious.

"Say, what's the big idea?" I asked.

Fred said, "Now listen, Pint-Size, we're going to have to put a bandage over your eyes so you don't see so much it wouldn't be healthy. Now, if you'll just—"

I swung at him. He took my blow on the chin without appearing to have noticed it. His hand whipped out a folded bandage, put it down over my eyes. I fought and tried to shout. Fingers closed over my hands, handcuffs snapped around my wrists. The car began a lurching series of turns, designed to make me lose all sense of direction.

After a while I felt the slow jolt as it ran up into a private driveway. I heard a garage door open and close. The bandage was taken off. I was in a garage. The outer door closed, and a side door opened onto a flight of stairs. We climbed the stairs to a hallway, past a kitchen, through a dining room, and into a living room.

I kept up the pretense.

"What is this?" I asked. "I thought you were going to take me to the station."

"What station?"

"To see the chief."

"You're going to see the chief."

"But he isn't here?"

"Oh yes. He lives here."

"You're cops?" I asked.

The men looked at me with exaggerated surprise. "Cops?" they said. "Why, buddy, whatever gave you that idea? *We* never said we were cops. We simply said the chief wanted to see you. That's a nickname we have for the big shot, you know."

I figured there was no use in playing a part any more. I kept silent.

"Have a chair," the thickset man said. "The chief will be in right away. He'll ask you a few questions, then we'll drive you back up town, and everything will be all hunky-dory."

I sat down in the chair and waited. I heard quick, nervous steps in the corridor, and a fat individual, with blubbery lips and cheeks, who had perspiration smeared all over his forehead, came walking into the room with the quick, light step of a professional dancer. He was short, and he was pretty fat, but he stood straight as a ramrod, pushing his belly out in front of him; and his little short legs took quick, rapid-fire strides.

"The chief," the tall man said.

The chief smiled and nodded, his bald head bobbing on his fat neck like a cork bobbing on water. "Who is he, Fred?" he asked.

The man with the battered nose said, "He's with a gal by the name of Cool who runs a detective agency. They were employed to serve summons on Morgan Birks in the divorce action. He was hanging around the Perkins Hotel."

"Oh yes. Oh, yes," the chief said, rapidly, bobbing his head and smiling affably. "Yes, indeed. Pardon me for not recognizing you. And what's your name?"

"Lam," I said. "Donald Lam."

"Yes, yes, Mr. Lam. I'm certainly glad to meet you, and it was very nice of you to come out, very nice indeed. Now tell me, Mr. Lam, you're working for—what was the name, Fred?"

"Bertha Cool—the Cool Detective Agency."

"Oh yes. You're working for the Cool Detective Agency."

I nodded.

"How long have you been with them?"

"Not very long."

"Find it congenial employment?" he asked.

"So far."

"Yes, yes. I dare say it's a nice opening for a young man, plenty of opportunities to use intelligence, ingenuity, and quick wit. I would say there was quite an opportunity to work up. I think you've displayed very commendable judgment, very commendable judgment, indeed, in getting into work of that kind. You look alert and intelligent."

"Thank you," I said.

His head bobbed up and down, the fat on his neck wash-boarding into wrinkles, and the coarse hair on the back of his neck bristled and wriggled like the hairs on a flexible brush.

"Now when did you see Morgan Birks last?" he bubbled.

"I make my reports to Mrs. Cool," I said.

"Yes, yes, of course. How careless of me."

A door opened, and a big woman came in. She wasn't fat, just big; broad-shouldered, big-hipped, and tall. She was dressed in a gown which showed the gleaming skin across her broad shoulders, the sweep of her heavy neck, the well-muscled arms.

"Well, well, well," the fat man said. "Here's the little woman! So glad you could drop in on us, Madge. I was just asking Mr. Lam about Morgan Birks. Pet, this is Donald Lam. He's a detective, working with the—what was that name, Fred?"

"The Cool Detective Agency."

"Oh yes. Working with the Cool Detective Agency," the fat man said. "And what's the name of the woman that runs it, Fred?"

"Bertha Cool."

"Yes, yes, that's right. Bertha Cool. Sit down, m'love, and see what you make of it. Mr. Lam, this is my wife."

I knew I was in a jam. Sometimes a man doesn't lose anything by being polite, no matter how the cards are stacked. I got to my feet, and bowed from the waist. "I am very pleased to meet you," I said, and tried to make my voice sound as though I meant it.

She didn't say a word.

"Sit down, Lam. Sit down," the fat man said. "You've doubtless had a hard day. You detectives have quite a bit of running around to do. Now, let's see, Lam. Where were we—oh yes, you'd been given papers to serve on Morgan Birks, hadn't you?"

"I think you'd better get in touch with Mrs. Cool if you want to find out about these things."

"Cool—Cool? Oh yes, the woman who runs the detective

agency. Well, that's a splendid idea, Lam, but you see, we're a bit pressed for time, and we don't know just where the lady is. But *you're here,* and doubtless you have the information."

I didn't say anything.

"Well, now," the fat man said. "I hope you're not going to be obstinate, Mr. Lam. I certainly *do* hope you're not going to be obstinate."

I remained silent. The man with the battered face moved a step closer.

"Now just a minute, Fred," the chief said. "Don't get impulsive. Let's let Mr. Lam tell this in his own way. Don't bother to interrupt him. Don't try to hurry him. Now let's just begin at the beginning, Mr. Lam."

I said courteously, "Would you mind telling me just what you want to know, and why you want to know it?"

"Now *that's* the spirit," the chief said, beaming all over his face, his little protruding gray eyes looking for all the world as though they'd been crowded out by the layers of fat which had been deposited on his cheeks. "That's exactly the spirit! We'll tell you anything you want to know, and you tell us what we want to know. You see, Mr. Lam, we're business men. We've been associated with Morgan Birks, and Morgan Birks has certain—well, you might call them liabilities—certain obligations to us. We don't want him to forget those obligations. We're anxious to see that he's reminded of them. Now you're employed to serve papers, and we wouldn't interfere with that for anything on earth, would we, Fred? Would we, John? That's right. The boys agree with me. We wouldn't interfere with your work at all, Mr. Lam; but *after* your work is finished, we want to know where Mr. Birks is."

"Well," I said, "I see no reason why I can't help you—*if* Mrs.

Cool says it's all right. Of course, she's my boss, and I wouldn't want to do anything without her."

The tall man said, "You'd better let Fred soften him up a bit, Chief. From all we can figure, things are getting hot. It looks as though he'd expected Morgan Birks at the Perkins Hotel. The whole gang moved in there. Sandra Birks, her brother who came out from the East—and had his nose broken in an automobile accident, a bird who said at the desk his name was Holoman, who doesn't figure in the picture anywhere that we can see, Alma Hunter, Bertha Cool, and this guy. He took Bertha Cool out of the hotel and put her in a taxicab. He was turning around to go back to the hotel when we picked him up."

The chief said, "You'd better tell us, Mr. Lam, because it's really important to us, and sometimes my boys get impulsive. No one deplores it more than I do, but you know how boys are. They just *will* be boys!"

"I think Mrs. Cool would gladly co-operate with you," I said, "if you'd get in touch with her. And I think she has information that would be valuable to you. You understand, she's in the business of getting information and selling it to clients."

"That's right, so she is," the fat man said. "Well now, *that's* a thought! It is, for a fact! I'll have to take that up with the little woman. What do you think of it, m'love?"

The big woman didn't change expression by the twitching of a muscle. Her hard, cold eyes looked at me as though I'd been a specimen under a microscope. "Soften him up," she said.

The big man nodded.

Fred shot out his arm with the speed of a striking snake. His fingers hooked around the knot in my necktie, twisted it until it started choking me. He pulled on the necktie, and I came up out of the chair as though I hadn't weighed fifty pounds. "Stand up," he said. His right hand swung up from his hips so that the heel of his palm pushed the tip of my nose back into my face and sent tears squirting out of my eyes. "Sit down," he said.

Under the impact of that hand, I went down like a sack of meal. "Stand up," he said, and his hand on my necktie brought me up.

I tried to get my hands up to block the heel of his hand as it came for my sore nose. He speeded up the punch just a little, and beat me to it. "Sit down," he said.

I felt that the whole front of my face was coming off.

"Stand up."

"Sit down."

"Stand up."

"Sit down."

"Stand up."

"Sit down."

"Talk."

He stepped back a pace and let go of me.

"Talk," he repeated, "and don't take too long about it." His face was expressionless. His voice held a note of impersonal boredom as though he'd been softening people until it had become a routine chore, and he felt aggrieved about being called upon to perform it after five o'clock.

"That's right," the fat man said, nodding and smiling affably. "You see, Fred's right, Mr. Lam. When he says stand up, you stand up. When he says sit down, you sit down. Now then, when he says talk, you talk."

I groped for my handkerchief. There was blood trickling from my nose down the front of my face.

"Now, never mind that," the fat man said. "That's just a little surface leakage. As soon as you've told us what we want to know, you can go in the bathroom and get fixed up. Fred will help you. Now, when did you see Morgan Birks last?"

Unostentatiously, I swung around in the chair so that my leg was braced against it. "You," I said, "can go to hell."

The fat man held Fred back with a gesture of his upthrust palm. "Just a moment, Fred," he said, "don't get impulsive. The young man has spirit. Let's see what the little woman has to say. What do you think, m'love? Should we—"

"Go ahead," she said to Fred.

Fred reached for my necktie.

I came up out of the chair with everything I had and swung straight for his stomach. I pivoted from my hips so that my body muscles were behind the blow, my right fist traveling in a straight line with the force of a piston.

Something happened to my right arm. It went numb. A pile driver cracked me on the point of the jaw. I felt myself being lifted from my feet and sailing through the air. There were blinding flashes of light in front of my eyes and a feeling of black nausea in my stomach. I tried to get my eyes in focus, and saw a fist coming. Before I could do anything about it, the fist exploded into my face. From what seemed to be a far distance, I heard the woman's voice saying, "More in the ribs, Fred." And then something caved in the pit of my stomach. I doubled up like a jackknife and knew somehow that the thing which had banged against the side of my head and stayed there, was the floor.

I heard the fat man's voice sounding weak and fuzzy, like a blurred radio station. "Now take it easy, Fred. Don't overdo it. After all, you know, we want him to *talk*."

The tall man stood over me. He said, "Nuts on this guy. We're wasting valuable time. He's got the papers, and it's all arranged for him to serve them."

"Where's he got them?" the woman asked.

"In his inside coat pocket."

"Take a look," she said.

Fred reached over and poked his fingers in the collar of my shirt. He lifted me up so hard that my neck, which was like a dish rag, came back with a snap, and my head almost jerked off. I felt hands going through my pocket, first the inside pocket of my coat, then all of my coat.

Bill's voice made the report. "He's got the original summons. He hasn't any copies."

The woman said, "You damn fools. He's served them."

"He *couldn't* have served them," Fred said.

"What makes you think he couldn't?"

"I know he had them when he went to the Perkins Hotel. He was there about five minutes when Alma Hunter came in and joined him. They registered as man and wife. Then Sandra Birks and her brother showed up. Then he went out. He pulled the papers out of his pocket when he hit the sidewalk, to make sure they were all okay and ready for service, and pushed them back again into his inside coat pocket. He went to the telegraph office and sent a telegram. We don't know who it was to. The telegraph girls wouldn't kick through with any information. Money didn't interest them. We kept trying until they threatened to call the cops. I tagged him from there to a costumer's. He got a bellboy costume and went to the hotel. He was there about twenty minutes and then came out with Mrs. Cool."

"When did Mrs. Cool go to the hotel?" the chief asked.

"We didn't cover that. Jerry was on the job at the hotel. I think he said she came about twenty minutes before this guy went back with the costume."

I lay there on the floor, seemingly drifting on a sea of black pain with waves of nausea sweeping over me. I wanted to retch and couldn't. My sides hurt when I tried to breathe. I knew that the warm stuff trickling down my face and onto the collar of my shirt was blood, but I was too weak to do anything about it.

The woman said, "Get Jerry on the phone. Tell him to go through that hotel with a fine tooth comb. Morgan Birks is in there."

"Morgan Birks *can't* be in there," Fred kept insisting. "We had the tip on that hotel. Jerry's been on it ever since last week, and we know Birks hasn't been there—not yet. That hotel's the place where Morgan was to meet his cutie."

"Did you tail this guy, or pick him up at the hotel?" the woman asked.

"Picked him up at the hotel."

"And the hotel's sewed up?"

"Tighter than a drum."

"He served those papers in the hotel."

Someone reached down and picked me up. The end of my sore nose was clamped between the knuckles of two fingers. When the hand jerked, it felt as though my nose had come out by the roots. Fred's voice, still sounding bored, said, "Talk."

"Lay off his face, Fred," the woman said.

A kick at the base of my spine jarred me clean up to the top of my head. "Come on," Fred said, "give us the low-down. You served those papers."

I heard the ringing of a telephone bell. They all became silent. I heard pounding steps moving across the floor toward the bell. Then it ceased ringing, and the tall man's voice said, "Hello. Hello. . . . Who is it? Jerry? . . . Yes, Jerry. . . . Now listen, Jerry, we think he's there in the hotel. . . . I tell you he had them. . . . Of course, it's under an assumed name, and he's probably lying low. . . . Well, get through the room. Cover the dump. I tell you he's there. He has to be."

He hung up the telephone, and said, "About two minutes after we left, Sandra Birks, her brother, and Alma Hunter came out together. This other bird who doesn't enter the picture, came out. Jerry says he heard someone call him doctor. He thinks the brother had a hemorrhage, and the doctor was called in a rush to stop it. That's the best the boys could pick up."

I was coming back to consciousness again. The woman said, "Well, you can see what's happened. He's served those papers. He's delivered the copies, and is keeping the original on which to make his affidavit of service."

The big man said, "You wouldn't want to make a little easy money, would you, Mr. Lam?"

I didn't say anything. It was easier not to answer questions.

"If you wanted to pick up a little spot of cash, say five hundred dollars, or perhaps even six hundred dollars, I think it could be arranged. You could fix it so we could get Mr. Birks up here at the house. Perhaps you could arrange things—"

"Shut up," the woman interrupted in a level voice. "There's no dice with him. Don't be a damn fool."

The fat man said, "Well, you heard what the little lady said. I guess she's right at that. Feeling pretty bad, are you, Lam?"

I was feeling bad enough. As I got better, I got worse. That first pile-driving smash had knocked me half unconscious. Now, as the numbing effects of it commenced to wear off, I began to feel pain from the other beating.

The telephone rang again. "Answer it, Fred," the chief said.

Fred said, "Hello—yes—" and then was silent for almost two minutes. He said, "That's clever as hell," and was silent for another minute. Then he said, "Hold the phone," and came back into the living room. "News," he said. "Let's go where I can tell you."

The chief said, "You watch him, John."

I heard an exodus of steps and lay quiet, thinking how much my side hurt. After a while I heard Fred's voice on the telephone again. "All right. It clicks. I'll get on the job myself. G'by."

They came back into the room.

"Take him in the bathroom, Fred," the chief said, "and clean him up."

Fred picked me up as though I'd been a baby and carried me into the bathroom. He said, "Tough lines, Pint-Size, but it isn't as bad as though your nose had been broken. It'll be sore for a while, that's all. Here, let's get some cold water on it."

He set me on the toilet seat, let cold water run into the wash bowl, took my coat off, and started splashing cold wet towels on my forehead. My mind began to function more clearly. It got so I could focus my eyes.

He said, "That necktie's a mess. I guess we can find one of the chief's. Now how about that shirt? We can't use it. We'll have to do something about that. We can get the blood off the coat all right. Just a little cold water will fix that. Now, sit right still, and don't try to move around."

He got my shirt off, stripped me down to the waist, and sponged me with cold water.

I began to feel better.

The woman came into the bathroom, and said, "I think this shirt will fit him."

"We want a necktie," Fred said.

"I'll get one."

"And a bottle of alcohol and some smelling salts," Fred said. "We'll have him right as a rivet in five minutes."

The woman came back with smelling salts, alcohol, towels, a shirt, and tie.

Fred worked over me like a second ministering to a fighter between rounds. While he worked, he talked. "One good thing," he said, "you aren't bruised up any. That nose is going to be red for a while. It's going to be sore. Don't touch it. Don't try to blow it. Now then, a little alcohol on the back of the neck. There, that's fine. Let's slap a little over your chest—oh, that chest is sore, is it?—too bad. Nothing cracked, though, just a little wallop—you shouldn't have tried to hit me, Lam. Let me tell you something about hitting. When you're going to throw a right at a man, don't hook it around. And don't draw back your hand before you start a punch. I'm sorry you're so tender now, because you wouldn't take any interest in a lesson. But I could show you how to start a punch and the path a fist should travel, and in ten minutes it would make you about eighty per cent better when it comes to a fight. You've got what it takes. You've got guts, but you're too light to stand up against a punch. You'd have to learn to get away from 'em, and that takes foot work. Now then, let's put a little more alcohol on there—that's fine. The bleeding's stopped. That cold water's great stuff. Your hair will be wet for a while, but that won't hurt anything. Now then, on with the shirt—that's it. Now let's try the tie—rather a loud pattern to go with that suit, but it doesn't look bad at that."

The woman said, "Give him a shot of whisky, Fred."

"Brandy's better," Fred said. "Brandy will pick him right up. Get some of that seventy-five-year-old stuff, a big snifter of it. Don't be afraid of giving him too much. He's been knocked around a bit and it will take something to get him back to normal. He's a little bit light to take heavy punches like that. That one I hung on his jaw was pretty good. How is it, buddy? No teeth gone—that's fine. The jaw's sore, of course. It will be for a while."

Madge came back with a big snifter of brandy. Fred said, "This is the chief's favorite. He likes to dawdle around sipping it after meals, but you take it and gulp it right down. He says this is sacrilege, but you need it. Here we go, buddy."

I drank the brandy. It was smooth as sirup. It traced a hot streak down into my stomach, and then began radiating little branches of warmth which tingled along the nerves.

Fred said, "All right, up we go. Now we'll get that coat on, and into the car. Any particular place you want to be taken, buddy?"

I was weak and groggy. I gave him the address of my rooming house.

"What's that?" he asked.

"My rooming house."

"That's fine. We'll take you there."

I saw him exchange glances with the woman. Fred helped me up, and I walked out into the other room. The chief came walking toward me, his face wreathed in blubbery smiles. "Well, well," he said. "You certainly look a thousand per cent better, and that's a *mighty* becoming tie! Yes, sir! It certainly is. My wife gave me that tie for Christmas last year."

He threw back his head, and laughter bubbled forth. He quit laughing and grabbed my hand in his. He pumped it up and down and said, "Lam, you were splendid! You've got plenty of nerve my boy plenty of nerve. You've got what it takes. I wish I had a few men like you. You don't feel like telling us anything?"

"No," I said.

"I can't blame you, my boy. I can't blame you a bit."

He kept pumping my arm. "Take him wherever he wants to

go, Fred," he said, "and be careful with him. Don't drive too fast. Remember he's sore. All right, Lam, my boy, perhaps I'll see you later. Who can tell? No hard feelings, Lam. Tell me there's no hard feelings."

"No hard feelings," I said. "You beat me up, and God damn you, if I ever get a chance to get even I'll pour it to you."

For a minute his eyes hardened. Then he bubbled into effusive laughter. "That's the spirit, my boy, the old fighting spirit! Head bloody but unbowed, and all that sort of stuff. Too bad he hasn't a little more beef, Fred. He'd have given you a tussle for a fact. He came up out of that chair as though he'd been shot from a gun."

"Aw, he was awkward, and he couldn't swat a fly hard enough to hurt it," Fred said, "but he has guts, that boy."

"Well, take him up town. Just be certain that he doesn't try to locate the house so he can find his way back to it. You know, Lam, it's been a nice visit, and we don't want to seem inhospitable, but if you come back here again we'd much rather you came with *us* than with someone else."

And he roared with laughter at his own joke.

Fred said, "Come on, buddy. Put this handkerchief over your eyes, and away we go."

He blindfolded me, and he on one side, the chief on the other, led me back through the hallway, down the stairs, and into the car. A garage door went up and I shot out into the night. The fresh air felt good on my face. After we'd been riding about five minutes, Bill took off the blindfold and said, "Just settle right back against the cushions, Lam. I'll drive slow."

He was a skillful driver, and he threaded the car through traffic until he came to my rooming house. I saw him looking it over. He parked the car, opened the door, and helped me up the steps. Mrs. Smith opened the door, and looked at me. Her look was eloquent. A roomer who hadn't been able to pay rent for five weeks being brought home drunk.

Fred said, "Now don't look like that, madam. The boy's all right. He's been shaken up in an automobile accident, that's all. He'll want to go up to his room and lie down."

She came closer and sniffed my breath. "That certainly *was* an automobile accident," she said. "He must have run into a truckload of whisky."

"Brandy, ma'am," Fred said. "The very choicest seventy-five-year-old brandy. That was a shot of the chief's private stock given to him to brace him up."

"I got a job today," I told her.

I saw her eyes lighten. "How about the rent?" she asked.

"Next week," I said, "when I get paid."

She sniffed and said, "A job. I suppose you're celebrating."

I fumbled around in my pocket and produced the certificate of appointment as a private investigator which Bertha Cool had given me. She looked it over, said, "A private detective, huh?"

"Yes."

"Well, I wouldn't think much of you as a detective."

Fred said, "Now don't be too sure, ma'am. He's got nerve, that boy has. He'll make a success in anything. He has plenty of what it takes. Well, good night, Lam. I'll be seeing you again one of these days."

He turned and went down the stairs. I said to Mrs. Smith, "Quick, get the license number on that automobile," and as she hesitated, added, "He owes me some money. I can pay the room rent if I get it."

With that incentive she walked out to stand on the porch.

Fred went away from there with a rush. She came back and said, "I'm not certain. The number was either 5N1525 or 5M1525."

I fumbled around until I found a pencil, wrote both numbers down on a piece of paper, and hobbled up the three flights of stairs. She stood looking after me and said, "Don't forget it, Mr. Lam, I can use that room-rent just as soon as you get it."

"I won't," I told her. "I don't think I'll ever forget it."

CHAPTER SEVEN

A STEADY, insistent pounding on my door dragged me from oblivion into stupefied semi-consciousness. I heard the voice of my landlady saying, "Mr. Lam—oh, Mr. Lam—Mr. Lam. Get up."

I reached out for the light. My body felt as though it would break in two. I found the light, switched it on, and limped to the door of the little attic bedroom.

The landlady had on a faded green wrapper which made her look like sacked potatoes. The white fringe of a flannel night-gown burst out from beneath the wrapper. She said in a voice shrill with indignation, "I don't know what this new job of yours is, but I've put up with just about enough! I've let you get weeks behind with room rent, and now—"

"What is it?" I interrupted, and when I tried to talk my swollen nose and lips made my face feel wooden.

"It's a woman on the telephone who says she has to talk with you. She keeps screaming into my ear that it's a matter of life and death. The phone's been ringing and ringing and ringing. It's woke up everyone in the house. And *I've* had to climb three flights of stairs and stand here banging on the door until—"

"I'm much obliged, Mrs. Smith," I said.

"Obliged, eh?" she sniffed. "Great goings on to wake every-one up and—"

I forced my tortured body into action, dove back into the room, grabbed a bathrobe, flung it over my pajamas, and kicked my feet into slippers. It seemed an interminable distance down the hall. Alma was all I could think of. I hoped it was Bertha Cool with some new assignment. I knew she was quite capable of doing that very thing, but—The receiver was dangling from the cord. I grabbed it up, placed it to my ear, said, "Hello," and heard Alma's voice. "Oh, Donald, I'm *so* glad I reached you. Something awful's happened."

"What?"

"I can't tell you over the phone. You must come."

"Where are you?"

"I'm in the telephone booth in the lobby of Sandra's apartment house."

"Well, where will I meet you?" I asked.

"I'll be right there."

"In the apartment, you mean?"

"No—in the telephone booth. Something awful's happened. Come quickly."

I said, "Right away," hung up the telephone, and went up the stairs as fast as I could force my sore muscles into action. I passed Mrs. Smith wheezing down the steps. She said acidly, "There *are* people in the house, Mr. Lam, who are trying to get *back* to sleep."

I got to my room, flung off my robe and pajamas, climbed into my clothes, and was tying my necktie as I dashed down the stairs to the street. I buttoned my vest on the way to the corner. It seemed an age before a late-cruising taxicab came prowling along close to the curb. I signaled him and gave him the address. In the cab, I asked, "What time is it, buddy?"

"Half past two."

My wrist watch hadn't been good enough to pawn, but by setting it every day, I could approximate the time. Now it was on the dresser by the head of my bed. I looked through my pockets to make sure I had the certificate of appointment as a private detective which Bertha Cool had given me. I scooped the silver out of my pocket, and held it in the palm of my hand, counting it against the flicking figures which appeared on the illuminated dial of the taximeter. When the driver stopped at the address, there was five cents over. I handed him the whole collection of coins, said, "Thanks a lot, buddy," and made a dive for the door. I almost broke my. arm. It was locked tight. The lobby was lighted, but there was no one at the little desk. I kicked against the door, hoping that Alma would hear me. She did after a while, and came out of the telephone booth and down the corridor.

I stared at her in surprise. She had on sheer silk pajamas, and some sort of a filmy gown over them. She opened the door, and I said, "Alma, what's happened?"

"I've shot someone," she said, in a hoarse whisper.

"Who?"

"I don't know."

"Did you kill him?"

"No."

"Have you notified the police?"

"No."

"All right, then," I said. "We notify the police right away."

"But Sandra wouldn't want me to, and Bleatie says—"

"To hell with Sandra and Bleatie both," I said. "Get in there and telephone the police."

I piloted her back to the telephone booth.

"Donald, don't you think I'd better tell you what—"

"If you've shot anyone," I said, "you get in touch with the police and tell them the whole story."

She turned to me and said, "I'll have to ask you for a nickel."

I went through my pockets. There wasn't a coin on me. I'd given my last cent to the cab driver. I tried the telephone. It simply, positively, wouldn't work without the coin.

"How did you telephone me?" I asked.

She said, "A man came in. He was drunk. I told him a story about my husband locking me out, and asked him for a coin so I could telephone. He gave me a nickel."

"All right. Let's go back up to the apartment."

"I can't. I haven't my keys. There's a spring lock on the door."

"We'll get the manager. Tell me, what happened?"

"I went to sleep, and woke up and someone was in the room. He was bending over the bed with his hand right over my nose, ready to shut off my breathing. After that awful experience of last night, I was almost paralyzed with terror. But you'd impressed on my mind what I was to do. You remember you said it didn't make any difference whether I hit him or not. So I jerked the gun out from under my pillow, and pulled the trigger. I'd slipped the safety catch off when I went to bed. I was never so frightened in my life. That gun made such an *awful* bang! I thought my eardrums would burst. I dropped the gun and screamed."

"Then what?" I asked.

"Then I grabbed a robe from the bed—I must have. I don't

remember doing it, but it was over my arm when I got out to the other room."

"You ran into the other room?"

"Yes, and then into the hall."

I said, "Well, he's probably in there now then, unless he managed to get out through a window. There's not one chance in ten that you hit him."

"Oh, but I *did* hit him," she said. "I heard an awful smack like a bullet would make when it hit someone,—and he fell down."

"How do you know he fell down?"

"I heard him."

"Did you hear him move after that?" I asked.

"Yes, I think I did. I heard something. I went completely screwy. I dashed out into the corridor and ran for the elevator just as hard as I could run. The door closed and clicked shut behind me. I stayed in the elevator for a minute, and then realized what a predicament I was in. Look, I haven't even any slippers on."

I looked down at her tinted toenails, and said, "Well, we're going to have to get the manager. Don't be frightened, Alma. It's probably a burglar, someone who is looking for Morgan Birks' records, or thought, perhaps, he had some money salted away. Where was Sandra all this time?"

"She went out."

"Where was Bleatie?"

"I don't know. In bed, I guess, in the other room."

"And he didn't hear the shot?"

"I don't know."

"Look here, Alma," I said. "Do you suppose it could have been Bleatie who—"

"What would he be doing in my room?" she asked.

I couldn't think of any answer I wanted to put in words, so didn't try to give one. I said, "We'll find the manager, and—" I broke off and crowded her back into the telephone booth as a big car pulled up in front of the apartment house. "Here comes someone now," I said. "I can mooch a coin and call police headquarters. I'd rather do that than notify the manager."

"I have some money in my purse if we can get the door of the apartment open," Alma Hunter said.

"Well, we'll see who this is and—"

I could see the vague, indistinct form of a driver at the wheel of the big car. A girl was between him and me, and she almost smothered him saying good night. He didn't come around to open the car door for her or see her into the apartment. But as soon as she disentangled herself and opened the door of the car, he slid away from the curb and out into the night. I started toward the door and stopped. The woman was taking a latchkey from her purse. As she walked up to the door, I saw her face. It was Sandra Birks.

I walked back to the telephone booth and said, "Here comes Sandra now. You can go up with her. Tell me, Alma, how did it happen no one heard the shot?"

"I don't know."

"But you don't think they did?"

"No. At any rate, there hasn't been anything done about it."

Sandra Birks came in, walking with quick, determined little steps. Her cheeks were flushed, and her eyes were starry. She seemed to be walking on air. I stepped out from behind the little counter which ran around the desk, and said, "Just a minute."

She caught her breath when she saw me, and then shifted her eyes to stare at Alma in her robe, pajamas, and bare feet.

"What's happened?" she asked.

"If you've got a nickel," I said, "we'll call the police. Alma shot someone in your apartment."

"Who?"

"A burglar," Alma said, quickly.

"The same one who—" Sandra broke off to look at her throat. Alma nodded. "I think so."

"Where did you get the gun?"

I started to say, "I gave it to her," but Alma said quickly, "It was one I had. I'd had it in Kansas City. I kept it in the bottom of my suitcase."

Sandra said, "We'd better go up and look things over before we—"

"No, we hadn't," I interrupted. "There's been enough delay already. We call the police."

Sandra said, "What's the matter? Haven't you a nickel?"

I met her eyes, and said, "No."

She opened her purse, took out a nickel and gave it to me. I walked back to the telephone booth. Sandra and Alma stood there by the elevator, talking in low tones; and just then I heard the low wail of a police siren, sounding close at hand. I was just taking the receiver off the hook in the telephone booth when a radio patrol car drew up in front of the door. I started dialing blind, stalling along to keep out of sight. An officer climbed the two stairs, tried the door, and rattled the knob. Sandra walked across and let him in. I could hear him say through the door to the telephone booth, "Someone reported a shot was heard in 419. Do you know anything about it?"

"I live there," Sandra Birks said.

"Oh, you do?"

"Yes."

"Was there a shot?"

"I just came in."

"Who's this dame?"

"She lives with me—it was a shot, I guess—she heard it."

"Let's go up."

He pushed them along with him into the elevator. The door rattled shut, and the elevator started swaying upward. Over the phone I heard the noise of the ringing bell and a sleepy masculine voice said "Hello." I thought for a moment, then put the receiver back on the hook.

Apparently no one had said anything about me.

I watched the indicator swing upward in an arc until it came to the fourth floor. Then it stopped. I waited a minute or two to see if the elevator was coming back down, and when I saw it wasn't, jabbed the button. The indicator remained stationary. Evidently, they'd left the door open when they went up. At that hour of the night, there was only one elevator running, and it was an automatic.

It took me a couple of minutes to climb the four flights of stairs and walk down the corridor to apartment 419.

The apartment door was open. I could hear the sound of voices coming from the bedroom on the right. The lights were on. I stepped into the apartment, and looked through the bedroom door. The two women were standing facing the officer: Alma Hunter, white-lipped, defiant; Sandra Birks, poker-faced. Sprawled on the floor with his arm outstretched, lying on his back, his glazed eyes reflecting the lights from the ceiling, lay Morgan Birks.

The officer asked Alma, "Where did you get this gun?"

"I had it."

"When did you buy it?"

"I didn't buy it."

"Who gave it to you?"

"A gentleman friend."

"Where? When?"

"In Kansas City, of course. It was some time ago. I don't remember how long ago."

Sandra Birks looked past the officer and saw me. Her eyes narrowed. She raised her hand to her lips, and as she lowered it, flipped the wrist in a signal to go away.

The officer caught either her motion or the expression in her eyes. He whirled and saw me standing there.

"Who's this?" he asked.

"What's happened?" I asked, staring down at the figure on the floor.

Sandra Birks said evenly, "I think he has an apartment somewhere on this floor."

The officer came pushing toward me. "You get out," he said. "This is a homicide. We don't want a lot of people trooping in. Who are you? What—"

"Why don't you put a sign on the door?" I said. "I thought there was some trouble here. You left the door wide open and—"

"All right," he said. "On your way, and we'll close it right now."

"Well, don't get hard about it. I have a perfect right to look in here when the door's open, and you can't keep me out. I'm not—"

"The hell I can't keep you out," he said, and clapped his big hand on my back between my shoulders. He wrinkled my coat up in his fingers to give him a good grip, and shoved. I went out in the hall so fast I had to put up my hand to keep from slamming into the wall on the other side of the corridor. Behind me, the door slammed shut, and I heard the lock click into place.

Cops are that way. If I'd tried to leave, he'd have dragged me in and given me the third degree. Getting hard and insisting that I had the right to stay, resulted in getting thrown out with no questions asked. He'd proved his point and established the superiority of a police officer over the poor dumb citizen who pays the taxes.

I didn't know just what had happened, but Sandra Birks' signal had been enough. I didn't need to have a brick house fall on me. I walked to the elevator and took it down. My ribs ached every time I breathed, and the shove the officer had given me hadn't helped any.

The radio patrol car was waiting at the curb. The second officer was seated in it, listening to broadcasts. He was taking notes as I came out, and looked up at me sharply; but the radio was blaring a description of a man wanted for something or other, and he let me go.

I tried to walk casually until I got to the corner, swinging out to the curb once or twice as though looking for a cruising cab. Behind me, I could hear the blare of the police radio as a voice said in a droning monotone, "—about thirty-seven or thirty-eight, height five feet ten inches, a hundred and eighty pounds, wearing a gray felt hat—wide black brim—shirt—tie spotted—red. When last seen—running—scene—crime—"

I turned the corner. A taxicab hove into sight. I flagged it.

"Where to?" the driver asked.

"Straight down the street," I said, "until I tell you to stop." It wasn't until we'd got half a dozen blocks that I suddenly realized I hadn't a cent to my name. I figured the meter would register about sixty-five cents getting to Bertha Cool's address. I gave him the number and settled back against the cushions.

"Wait here," I said, and got out of the cab, crossed the curb to the apartment house, found Bertha Cool's name on the directory, and leaned against the door button.

There was going to be an embarrassing moment for me with that taxi driver if Bertha Cool wasn't in.

To my surprise, the buzzer sounded almost immediately. I pushed against the door, and it opened, letting me into a dark hallway. I groped around, found a light switch, and located the elevator. Bertha Cool was on the fifth floor. I had no difficulty finding her apartment. The light was on. She opened the door as I tapped on the panel. Her hair was messed from sleeping and hung in strings around her face. Her features looked bloated, but her eyes were cold and hard as diamonds glittering out at me from above the puffy folds of flesh. A silk bathrobe was knotted around her waist. Through the opening in the top, I could see the sweep of her massive throat, a V-shaped section of her big chest.

"You look like hell," she said. "Who beat you up? Come in."

I entered the apartment, and she closed the door. It was a two-room affair with a kitchenette opening from the back of the living room. The bedroom door was half open. I could see the bed with the covers thrown back, a desk telephone on a stand within a foot of the pillow, a pair of stockings thrown over the back of the chair, a wadded bundle of garments, which looked as though they'd been balled up and tossed onto the seat of another chair. The living room was close, and smelled of stale tobacco. She walked across to the windows, flung them open, looked at me sharply, and said, "What's the matter? Been run over by a truck?"

"Beaten up by mugs and pushed around by the police," I said.

"Oh, like that?"

"Yes."

"All right. Don't tell me about it until I've found the cigarettes. Where in hell did I put those things? I had a full pack when I went to bed—"

"In on the tabaret by the bed," I said.

She looked at me sharply, said, "You seem to have an observing disposition," dropped down in a big overstuffed chair, and went on in a calm, matter-of-fact voice, "Run in and get them for me, Donald. Don't try to talk to me until I've had a couple of good deep drags."

I brought her the cigarettes, held a match, and when she motioned toward an ottoman, slid it toward her. She elevated her feet, kicked off her slippers, twisted in the chair until she found a comfortable position, settled herself, and said, "Go ahead."

I told her everything I knew.

She said, "You should have telephoned me before you went to bed. You should have let me know right away."

"But he hadn't been killed then," I said. "I only got the phone call—"

"Oh, the murder," she interrupted. "To hell with the murder. The police can take care of that, but this gang that kidnaped you and wanted to get in touch with Morgan Birks sounds like ready money to me. You passed up a bet there. You—" The telephone rang.

She sighed. "Donald, go get me that telephone. You can pull the jack out and plug it in here. There's a long extension cord on it. Hurry before they hang up, dear."

I ran into the bedroom, followed the extension cord to the wall plug, pulled it out, handed the telephone to Mrs. Cool, and plugged into the living room connection.

She picked up the receiver, said, "Bertha Cool talking," and waited.

I could hear the rattle of the diaphragm in the receiver as words poured into Bertha Cool's ear. The twinkling eyes indicated she was enjoying the conversation.

"What do you want *me* to do?" she asked at length.

The receiver made more noise, and Bertha Cool said, "I'd want five hundred dollars, cash money. After that, I'll probably want more. I can't guarantee anything. . . . Well, you'll have to get it, dearie. . . . Safety deposit boxes mean nothing to me. They'll seal them anyhow. . . . All right, dearie. Fifty dollars will be all right until tomorrow. . . . I'll keep him under cover. Yes, I hadn't better come over there right away. Wait until the police get done. There's no need of antagonizing them. What time is it now? . . . All right. Let's say an hour or an hour and a half. You wait there for me unless they take you to headquarters. I don't think they will."

She hung up, and her lips twisted in a smile of satisfaction.

"Sandra Birks," she said.

"Wants you to investigate her husband's death?"

"Wants me to take care of Alma Hunter. They're arresting her."

"They got a crust!" I said. "He was trying to choke her, and—"

"Don't be so sure," she said. "Morgan Birks was shot in the back."

"*In the back!*" I exclaimed.

"Uh huh. He was evidently trying to get out the door when he was shot. The bullet went completely through and imbedded itself in the door. Reconstructing the position of the body from the direction of the wound, the police figure he had his hand on the doorknob and was trying to get out when he was shot in the back."

"Well, what the devil business did he have coming in her room, anyway? What was he looking for?"

"A drink of water probably," she said. "But the police don't like to have girls shoot men in the back and then claim they were being attacked."

"It was dark in the room," I said.

"He was trying to get out."

"He'd tried to choke her the night before."

"*He* had?"

"Yes."

"Tell me about it."

I told her. She listened carefully and said, "How does she know it was Morgan Birks who tried to choke her?"

"It stands to reason," I insisted.

"It takes more than that to sell the police on an idea," she said. "Donald, be a good boy. Ring up the motor-vehicle registration department at headquarters, tell them it's the Cool Detective Agency, and get them to give you the registration of 5N1525 and 5M1525. I'm going to go get some clothes on."

She pinched out the cigarette, exhaled a long last appreciative cloud of smoke, heaved herself from the chair, and strode out toward the bedroom, removing the silk robe as she walked. She dressed without bothering to close the door. I couldn't see her, but I could hear her moving around; and she could hear me as I called the department of vehicular registrations and found out that 5N1525 was registered in the name of George Salisbery, 938 Main Street, Centerville, and 5M1525 in the name of William D. Cunweather, 907 Willoughby Drive.

I hung up the telephone after writing down the names and

addresses, and Mrs. Cool called from the bedroom, "That Salisbery guy doesn't sound so good. That Willoughby Drive address may be our meat. How does it seem to you, Donald?"

"It could be. The house looked as though it were out around that section somewhere."

"Call a cab," she said.

"I have one waiting downstairs."

"Are you sporting taxicabs for your private transportation?" she asked. "Or did you think you were on an expense account?"

I flared up and said, "I thought I was on an expense account."

She was silent for several seconds. I sat there wondering whether she was going to blow up and fire me or take it.

"All right," she said in that maternal voice of hers. "We'll go downstairs and take it, Donald, dear. I'll make a note of whatever's on the meter and take it out of your salary. Let's go."

CHAPTER EIGHT

The taxi driver turned into the eight hundred block on Willoughby Drive. Mrs. Cool said, "Go down to 907, but don't stop. Drive past slowly and let us look it over."

The driver asked no questions. Fares who send a cab prowling around at that hour of the morning are apt to make peculiar requests, and a cab driver gets his tips by saving his arguments until he gets home to his wife.

"Take a look at it, Donald," she said, as the driver indicated the house on the corner.

I studied the driveway leading into the garage, figured the general layout of the house, and said, "That *could* be it."

"You're not certain?"

"No."

"Well," she said, "it's a hell of a chance, but we'll give it a try. Swing around to the curb, driver, and stop at that house across the street—the one on the corner."

The cab driver swung the car to a stop. "Want me to wait?" he asked.

"Yes, wait," she said.

I held the door open. She pulled the springs far over as she stepped to the ground, disdaining our assistance. The driver stood and watched us go up the cement walk toward the dark, silent house. I groped for the bell button, found it, and leaned against it. Inside the house, I could hear the jingling of the bell.

"Do I do the talking, or do you?" I asked.

"If it's the right party," she said, "tip me off. Let me go on from there."

"All right," I said, "but if someone I've never seen before comes to the door, we'll have to get in the house before I can be certain."

"All right. Tell them I'm sick, and you want to come in and telephone for a doctor—you've seen the room where the telephone's located, haven't you?"

"One of the phones, at any rate."

"All right. That's all we need—don't keep that thing going so steadily, Donald. Take it easy. Let up, and ring again after a minute or two."

I could hear someone moving around on the upper floor. A window raised, and a masculine voice said, "Who is it?"

"It sounds like the chief's voice," I whispered.

Bertha Cool raised her voice and said, "I have an important message to deliver here."

"Put it under the door."

"It isn't that kind of a message."

"Who are you?"

"I'll give you the name when you come down," she said.

For a second or two the man seemed undecided, then he slammed the window down. A light clicked on, and the window blazed into an oblong of brilliance that was subdued as the shade was pulled. A second or two later I heard steps on the stairs.

"Move over to one side, Donald," she said. "Let me stand in front of the door."

The porch light clicked on, flooded us with brilliance. Bertha Cool stood squarely in front of the oval plate glass window in the front door. The steps had ceased now, and I had the impression that someone was looking through the window, sizing her up.

After a moment, the door opened a crack, and the man said, "What is it?"

I stepped back and around so I could see him. It was the chief. He was wearing light silk pajamas and slippers, with no robe.

I said, "Hello, chief."

He stiffened for a minute into ominous, tense immobility. Then his fat, blubbery lips twisted into a smile. He said, "Well, well, well, it's Lam! I hadn't expected to see you so soon, Lam. I hadn't expected you'd find your way back so quickly. And who's your friend?"

"Bertha Cool," I said, "head of the Cool Detective Agency."

"Well, well, well," the chief beamed. "This is indeed a pleasure, and I want to congratulate you—er—er—is it Miss or Mrs.?"

"Mrs.," she said. "Mrs. Bertha Cool."

"It's indeed a pleasure." He bowed. "And you're to be congratulated on having a man so quick-witted and courageous as Lam working for you. He's a bit of all right, that boy! A most observing disposition; and I can personally vouch for his courage. Do come in."

He stood to one side. I hesitated, but Mrs. Cool sailed past me through the door and into the reception hall. I followed her.

The chief slammed the door shut, and shot a bolt into place. "So you found your way back, Lam?"

I nodded.

"I'll have to speak to Fred about that. I will indeed. That was rather a faux pas on his part, letting you get the address. Would you mind telling me just how you did it, Mr. Lam?"

Bertha Cool answered the question. "Yes, he would," she said.

"Well, well, well, no hard feelings," the chief said. "Won't you come in and sit down—sorry I can't offer you a drink."

He switched on lights in the living room and we went in and sat down.

A woman's voice from the head of the stairs called down, "Who is it, dear?"

"Come down, m'love. Slip on something and come down. We have a couple of visitors. You know one, and I'm quite anxious to have you meet the other."

He beamed across at Mrs. Cool, and said, "Always like to have the little woman in our conferences. You know how it is. I believe marriage is a partnership, and two heads are always better than one. Whenever the situation becomes just a little delicate, I always call in the little woman."

I heard a door slam up above, and then the stairs began to creak. We followed the creak on down until the tall woman came silently into the room, walking on the felt soles of bedroom slippers.

She didn't pay any attention to me. Her eyes were fixed on Bertha Cool's.

I got up when she came in. The chief didn't. I said, "Mrs. Cunweather—is that the name?"

The fat man hastened to say, "It will do just as well as any,

Lam, my boy. After all, what's in a name? Yes, yes, let it be Cunweather by all means. Mrs. Cunweather, my wife, Mrs. Cool. I want you two to be friends."

The tall, big woman looked down at the chunky one. Mrs. Cunweather said, "How do you do, Mrs. Cool?" And Mrs. Cool said, "Howdy do. I hope you don't stand on formality—I don't."

Mrs. Cunweather sat down. Her eyes were cautious—watchful.

The chief said, "Precisely what do you want, Mrs. Cool?"

"Money," Bertha Cool said.

His face broke into blubbery smiles. "Well, well, well, Mrs. Cool. That's being direct! That's a woman after my own heart. I've always said that I like plain, straightforward business where there's no beating about the bush, haven't I, m'love?"

He didn't turn toward his wife as he spoke. Evidently, he expected no reply from her, and she made none.

Mrs. Cool said, "I thought we'd talk terms."

"Now, don't get me wrong," the fat man said. "I don't know what Mr. Lam has told you, but if he insinuates that he received other than the most courteous treatment at my hands, he—"

"Nuts," Mrs. Cool said. "We're not wasting time over that. You beat him up—it's good for him—toughen him up some. Beat him up again if you want to, only don't leave him so he can't go to work at eight-thirty in the morning. I don't give a damn *how* he spends his evenings."

The chief broke into laughter. "Well, well, well," he said, "if you aren't a quaint, original woman—that is, if you don't mind my saying so. That's being delightfully frank. Now tell me, just what was it you had in mind, Mrs. Cool?"

"You want to know about Morgan Birks. I might be able to tell you something."

"Well, well, well, that's nice of you, Mrs. Cool. We certainly appreciate that, my wife and I. And it was nice of you to drive out here early in the morning and tell us. After all, you know, sometimes seconds are important in this business, and we hate to lose them. Now precisely what was it you had to offer, Mrs. Cool?"

Mrs. Cool said, "We served papers on Morgan Birks."

"Oh, you served them."

"Of course we served them."

"Do you know," the man said, "I insisted all along that Donald had served them. And so did the little woman. You served them somehow in the hotel, didn't you, Donald?"

"Don't answer, Donald."

"I'm not going to," I said.

The chief turned to his wife. "There you are, m'love," he said, "perfect teamwork. That's what comes of doing business with people who appreciate the possibilities of a situation.

"Well, well, well, Mrs. Cool. I don't know just what to say. You say that we want Morgan Birks. That isn't at all correct, and yet it's the way it would doubtless appear to a person running a detective agency. But let's concede, just for the sake of the argument, that we would like to have a few words with Morgan Birks—what of it?"

"How much is it worth?"

"Well now," the fat man said, stroking his chin, "this is a rather unusual proposition."

"And rather unusual circumstances," Bertha Cool reminded him.

"Yes, yes, that's right. It is for a fact—I can't get over Donald finding this place so promptly. It's rather uncanny, you know. I had thought that all the necessary precautions had been taken."

Bertha Cool said, "I know where Morgan Birks can be found. You can't talk with him. Is that information worth anything to you?"

The smile froze on the chief's face. Above the curved lips, his eyes were hard and watchful.

"You mean he's in jail?"

"I mean you can't talk with him."

"He's been drinking again?"

"I can tell you where he is."

"How much do you want?" the chief asked.

"Whatever it's worth."

"Why can't I talk with him?"

Bertha Cool said, "I don't want to take an unfair advantage."

"You mean he's dead?"

"I can tell you where he is."

The fat man looked at his wife. She shook her head. The gesture was all but imperceptible.

The chief turned back to Bertha Cool. He seemed more relaxed now. "No," he said, "the information wouldn't be worth anything to me. I'm sorry, Mrs. Cool, because I think you have a great deal of ability. And I'm positively fond of Lam. I really am. Perhaps some day I can hire your agency. There might be some information you could get for us."

Cunweather turned back to his wife, and said, "What do you think, m'love? Don't you think Mr. Lam is a bright young man?"

Mrs. Cunweather said, tonelessly, "Fred was driving the sedan when he took Lam back to his room. Lam got a look at the license number."

Cunweather's headshake was emphatic. "I don't think he did, m'love. When I told Fred to take the sedan, I cautioned him about that. I told him to switch out the lights when he parked the car, deliver Mr. Lam to his room, and not switch on the car lights until he was certain Lam was where he couldn't see."

"That's how Lam found this place," Mrs. Cunweather said in a tone of flat finality.

The chief pinched his pendulous lower lip between his thumb and forefinger. "I hope Fred isn't getting careless," he said. "I do, indeed. I'd hate to lose Fred. That's the worst of a man who has a great deal of physical prowess. He underestimates men who are not as strong as he is. I think Fred always underestimates the other man's mentality, don't you, m'love?"

"We'll talk about Fred later," she said. "Right now we're talking about hiring Mrs. Cool and Mr. Lam."

"Leave me out of it," I said.

Mrs. Cool said, "Don't pay any attention to Donald. He's working for me. I'm giving the orders. What's your proposition?"

"I don't know that we have any," Cunweather said.

His tone lacked finality, and Bertha Cool didn't take the answer as final. She continued to sit there, waiting. Cunweather glanced once more at his wife, twisted his underlip into a weird shape. "I'll be frank with you, Mrs. Cool," he said. "We're in a position where time is precious. Seconds may count. We need help to get certain information. I think you have some of the information we want. We might talk a while."

"You talk," she said. "I'll listen."

"No, that won't do at all. We'd have to exchange information."

Bertha Cool said, "I don't want any of your information. If you want some of mine, it's going to cost you money."

"Yes, yes. I understand," Cunweather said. "But in order to determine how extensive your information is and how much it might be worth to us, we'd have to talk things over."

"Go ahead and talk," Bertha Cool said, shifting her weight in the chair in search of a more comfortable position.

Cunweather said, "We don't want Morgan Birks now. We do want information about Morgan Birks. We're particularly interested in knowing about Morgan's sweetheart. My men slipped up on that, and slipped up badly. I knew that there was to be a play at the Perkins Hotel. I knew Morgan was scheduled to meet someone there. I didn't know when. I didn't know whom. Apparently the woman we wanted was registered as Mrs. B. F. Morgan. Now my men were so busy looking for Morgan Birks they didn't pay much attention to that woman. She gave us the slip."

Cunweather paused to give Mrs. Cool a chance to talk. She didn't say anything.

"We'd like very much to know more about Mrs. B. F. Morgan," Cunweather said.

"How much do you want to know, and what's it worth?"

"We'd like to know where we could find her."

"I could help on that," Bertha Cool said.

"Could you put your finger on her?"

"Yes."

Cunweather glanced again at his wife. She maintained a stony stare of silent attention. When Cunweather failed to receive any signal, he turned to Mrs. Cool. "Well now," he said, "that *would* help. Of course, Mrs. Cool, I'll be frank with you; one of our objections to hiring outside help is that they sometimes try to do a little chiseling on the side. We don't like that. I think Mr. Lam has told you it isn't healthy to try to chisel on us."

Bertha Cool said, "Don't try to frighten me. My health is *very* good. I have a damn strong constitution."

"Ha! ha! ha!" Cunweather laughed. "That's good! A strong constitution. Yes, Mrs. Cool, I'm satisfied you have. I like the way you handle yourself. I think we could offer you employment."

Mrs. Cool said, "When I leave here, I'm going to see Sandra Birks. If you want me to work for you and there's enough money in it, I'll work for you. If Sandra Birks wants me to work for her and there's enough money in it, I'll work for her. I want to pick the job that offers the most money."

"You mean you want me to make an offer?"

"Yes."

"And then you want to see Mrs. Birks and see what she has in mind?"

"Yes."

"And accept the best offer?"

"Yes."

"I don't think I'd like that," Cunweather said. "I'm quite certain I wouldn't like it. I don't think it would be ethical."

"Don't lose any sleep worrying about *my* ethics," Bertha Cool said. "I'm putting cards on the table."

"Yes, I can see you are, Mrs. Cool—are you going to tell Sandra Birks that you had this chat with me?"

"That depends," she said.

"On what?"

"On what Sandra Birks wants me to do, and how much money there is in it."

"We wouldn't like you to mention that you were here. We'd consider it a violation of a confidence," Cunweather said.

"*I* wouldn't," Bertha Cool retorted. "You didn't invite me here. I found the place."

"You're making things rather difficult," Cunweather said.

Bertha Cool sighed, "We're doing a hell of a lot of talking without getting any place."

Cunweather said soothingly, "Look here, Mrs. Cool, I'm interested in your proposition, but I have to know a little more before I fix my price. I can't go it blind."

"What do you want to know?"

"I want to know that you can *really* put your finger on Morgan's sweetie. I want to know that you *really* served Morgan Birks, and weren't being victimized by a clever hoax."

"What do you mean by that?"

"Sandra Birks wanted a divorce. She had to serve papers on Morgan. She couldn't find Morgan, so she thought it might be clever to plant someone as Morgan Birks. You think Morgan Birks came to the Perkins Hotel today. We feel positive he didn't."

Mrs. Cool opened her purse, took out a cigarette, put it in her lips, groped around for matches, lit the cigarette, and said, "Tell him, Donald."

"What?" I asked.

"All about serving Morgan Birks. Keep talking until I tell you to stop."

I said, "Sandra Birks hired us. I went up to her apartment and got pictures of Morgan Birks. They were good snapshots. I checked up on them to make certain she hadn't planted some phonies in the album."

"Yes, I know," Cunweather said. "You're right on that. Those snapshots were in your pocket together with the original summons."

I said, "Sandra's brother, B. L. Thoms, whom she calls Bleatie, came out from Kansas City to—"

"From *where?*" Mrs. Cunweather interrupted.

"From Kansas City."

The chief glanced sharply at his wife. "Go on, Lam," he said.

"Bleatie came out to help Sandra. He knows Morgan Birks very well. I gather he's more friendly with Morgan than he is with his own sister. He said he'd give us a lead that would let us put the finger on Morgan Birks any time he was satisfied Sandra wasn't trying to double-cross Morgan. He didn't seem to have a particularly high opinion of his sister's morals or integrity."

I could see gleaming interest in the eyes of the fat man. Mrs. Cool said casually, "That's far enough, Donald. If we go on from there, it costs money."

"What do you mean money?" the fat man asked.

"Something," she said, "to pay for getting up at this hour of the morning. I'm running a detective agency. I have rent to pay, salaries to pay, a tax on my payroll, a federal income tax, an occupation tax to the city, and a state income tax on the money that's left after the federal people get done with my income. Then I have to pay a sales tax on all the clothes I buy and—"

"Yes, yes," he interrupted, smiling and bobbing his head with mechanical regularity, but keeping his turquoise green eyes fastened on Mrs. Cool. "I understand. I have problems of my own, Mrs. Cool."

"Well, I'm in the business of getting information and capitalizing on it," she said. "I have something you want. You tried to beat it out of my operative. I don't like that."

"We *were* a little abrupt, for a fact," the chief conceded.

"It costs me money to get my information. I don't pass it out for charity."

"I'm very much interested in that Perkins Hotel situation,"

the chief said. He said to his wife, "Do you suppose, m'love, that *we* could have had the double-cross?"

"Something screwy somewhere," she said.

"Should we say a hundred dollars to Mrs. Cool?"

The little woman nodded.

"One hundred dollars," the chief said.

"Make it two hundred," Bertha Cool said.

"A hundred and fifty," Mrs. Cunweather said to her husband, "and if she doesn't want that, give her nothing."

"All right," Bertha Cool said, "a hundred and fifty."

The fat man turned to his wife. "Do you happen to have a hundred and fifty, m'love?"

"No."

"My wallet is upstairs. Would you mind running up and getting it?"

"Take it out of your belt," she said.

He moistened his lips again, and said, "I'll tell you, Mrs. Cool, you go ahead and tell us, and I'll guarantee that you'll have the hundred and fifty. I'll promise it."

"You get the hundred and fifty," she said.

He sighed with resignation, got to his feet, and opened the top part of his pajamas. His belly was huge, white, and flabby. A chamois-skin money belt circled his middle. It had been soaked and discolored with perspiration. He opened one of the pockets and took out two hundred-dollar bills.

"That's the smallest you have?" Bertha Cool asked.

"That's the smallest."

"It's going to take nearly all of my small change."

"I'm sorry. That's absolutely the smallest."

Bertha Cool fished around in her purse, then looked hopefully at me. "Got any money, Donald?" she asked.

"Not a nickel," I said.

She counted out her money and said, "I have to save five dollars for the taxi bill. I've got forty dollars in change. I'll give you thirty-five. Call it square for that or you can go upstairs and get your wallet."

"We'll call it square for that," he said. "I wouldn't walk upstairs to save fifteen dollars."

"Bring over the two hundred, Donald," she said.

The fat man extended the money to me. I carried it over to Mrs. Cool. She gave me the change in one-dollar, five-dollar, and ten-dollar bills. I took them over to Cunweather. He passed them over to his wife. "Put that somewhere," he said. "I don't want that chicken-feed in my money belt." He closed the flap of his money belt, buttoned up his pajamas, tucked the coat down in the pants, looked across at me, and said, "Does Lam do the talking?"

"Lam does the talking," Mrs. Cool said.

I said, "Sandra gave Morgan Birks a—"

"Never mind that, Donald," she said. "That's betraying the interest of a client. Just tell him what happened about Morgan, how we found him, and how we served him. But don't tell him the name or address of Morgan's sweetie."

"Bleatie," I said, "gave me the name of Morgan's girl friend. I went to her and put on an act that we were going to drag her into the divorce action, and then shadowed the place. She led me to the Perkins Hotel She registered as Mrs. B. F. Morgan and got room 618. I bribed the bell captain to find out about what rooms were in the vicinity. He—"

"Yes, yes," Cunweather interrupted. "We know all about that, Donald. We know everything you did from the time you got to the Perkins Hotel."

"Then you know about serving Morgan Birks?" I asked.

"You didn't serve Morgan Birks—you served somebody else."

"The hell he did!" Bertha Cool interrupted. "He served Morgan Birks."

"Where?"

"In the girl's room—in 618."

Cunweather and his wife exchanged glances. "There's some mistake," Cunweather said.

"No, there isn't."

"Morgan Birks didn't go into room 618. We're absolutely positive of that."

"Don't worry. He was in there all right," Bertha Cool said. "I saw him myself."

"How about it, m'love," Cunweather said, turning to his wife, "shall we—"

"Let Donald finish his story," she said.

Cunweather looked back at me. "Go on with your story, Donald."

I said, "I got a room. Several people were with me. Sandra and Bleatie came in. Alma Hunter was there. I left them, and went out to a masquerade costume place, and got a bellboy's uniform that would fit me. I had a telegram addressed to Mr. B. F. Morgan, care of Western Union. I waited around until the telegram came in, signed for it, and wrote in lead pencil on the envelope, beside the address, 'Try Perkins Hotel.' Then I got a notebook, forged a few signatures in it, went up to the hotel, and found the party in a hell of a stew because Morgan Birks had come in shortly after I'd left. I changed to the bellboy's uniform, went out and knocked on the door of 618. When they wanted to know what it was, I said it was a telegram. They told me to shove it under the door. I shoved it far enough under the door so they could see the address, and that it was a telegram, but it was in the notebook, and the notebook was too big to go all the way under the door. I told them they had to sign a receipt. They fell for it and opened the door. I walked in, and Morgan Birks was lying on the bed. I served the papers on him. While I was doing that, Sandra got excited and came in. There was conversation back and forth. There was no question but what it was Morgan Birks."

The fat man glanced for confirmation at Bertha Cool.

"That's right," she said. "I saw him, and I've seen his pictures in the newspaper. It was the same man."

The fat man started rocking violently back and forth in the chair. Bertha Cool said, "The next time I have any information you want, don't try to get it by beating up one of my operatives. You get better service this way."

Cunweather said, "We didn't think Mr. Lam was going to be so difficult."

"My operatives are all tough," Mrs. Cool said. "I pick 'em that way."

Cunweather said, "Let me talk to my wife, Mrs. Cool. I think we can make you a proposition. How about it, m'love? Would you like to step in the other room for a minute?"

"Go ahead," Mrs. Cunweather said. "You're doing fine."

The chief turned back to Mrs. Cool. "We're interested in hiring your agency for one particular purpose," he said. "We want to get in touch with Morgan Birks' sweetie. We want to find out how many safety deposit boxes she rented in her name. We want to find out where they are. We want that information fast."

"How much is it worth?" Mrs. Cool asked.

"Suppose we say two hundred and fifty dollars for each box you tell us about."

"How many are there?" she asked.

"I don't know, Mrs. Cool, and that's a fact. Frankly, I'm not certain there are *any*, but I have my suspicions. I do indeed."

"No soap," she said. "I don't think I could make any money at it."

Cunweather said, "Now let's be reasonable about this, Mrs. Cool. You know where this woman is. You won't have to waste any time. Morgan Birks is pretty well hidden, and is going to stay pretty well hidden. He's just a little too smart for the police. He had his sweetie rent some safety deposit boxes. There may be five. There may be two."

"And there may not be any," Bertha Cool said.

"There you go again," Cunweather chuckled. "There's that unique personality of yours coming to the front. It's refreshing, but we aren't getting anywhere, and seconds are slipping through our fingers. Now there's Lam, a clever boy. He could go to this girl and have the information in no time."

I said, "Count me out."

Cunweather said, "Now, Lam, don't be like that. You're a nice boy. You should be more forgiving. After all, what happened tonight was just a matter of business."

"Forget Donald," Mrs. Cool said. "You make terms with me. I'll take care of Donald."

"We might make it three hundred dollars a box," Cunweather said.

"No."

"That's our limit."

Bertha Cool said, "I'll give you a ring and let you know—after I've talked with Sandra."

"We'd want your answer now."

"You have it."

Cunweather started rocking back and forth in his chair. Mrs. Cunweather said, "Ask her where Morgan Birks is now."

Cunweather said, "Come, come, Mrs. Cool. You've received a hundred and sixty-five dollars of my money. You know where Morgan Birks is. I think you should tell us."

She pursed her lips thoughtfully, and said, "That information might not do you any good. Again it might be worth money. I'm not one to give something for nothing."

The telephone rang while Cunweather was rocking back and forth thinking the thing out. "Would you answer it, m'love?"

"Answer it yourself," she said, sitting perfectly still.

He sighed, tightened his fingers around the arms of the rocking chair, heaved himself to his feet, and waddled out into the other room. He took the receiver off the hook, and said, in a cautious voice, "Yes, what is it?" After that, he was silent for eight or ten seconds. Then he said, "You're sure?—well, come on out here, and I'll give you some instructions. There's a new angle on the case."

He dropped the receiver into place without saying "good-by," came waddling back, and beamed at Mrs. Cool. "I can well appreciate how you feel, Mrs. Cool," he said. Then he turned to his wife and said, "Morgan Birks is dead, m'love. A girl named Alma Hunter shot him in Sandra Birks' apartment early this morning. She shot him in the back, just as he was trying to run from the apartment."

"Dead?" Mrs. Cunweather asked.

"Like a doornail," Cunweather assured her.

"That," she said, "makes it different."

Mrs. Cool said, "Come on, Donald."

I got to my feet. She closed her purse, slid her legs back so that her feet were as far in under the chair as she could get them, pushed her hands down against the arms of the chair, and got to her feet.

We started for the door. Cunweather and his wife were whispering. After a second or two, and before we were out of the hallway, Cunweather called, "Just a minute, Mrs. Cool. I want to ask you a question." He came waddling out into the hallway, and said, "Do you know whether Morgan Birks was in room 618 *all* the time? In other words, was he in there when this mistress of his registered?"

"I don't know," she said. "How about it, Donald?"

"No chance," I said, "unless she was standing in with the bellboy, and Morgan Birks had been planted there. The clerk rented her 618 as a vacant room. She'd telephoned and asked for two rooms with a connecting bath. She'd been assigned 618 and 20. When she registered, she gave up 620, saying the other party hadn't—" I broke off as something came to my mind.

"Hadn't what?" Cunweather asked, interested.

"Hadn't shown up. The bellboy took her up to 618. The captain got me the information, and I rented 620."

"Who had the bath?"

"I did."

"Then 618 had been rented without the bath?" Cunweather asked me.

I said, "I guess so—unless there was another bathroom between 618 and 616."

Mrs. Cunweather called from the other room, "Let her go, William. We've got enough information to handle it ourselves."

The chief said, "Well, Mrs. Cool, it's been most delightful having you drop in. *Do* come again some time. I'll remember you. I will for a fact—and don't hold a grudge, Lam. After all, my boy, you were splendid, and your nose doesn't look at all bad.

I can see from the way you're walking, your ribs are a bit sore, but you'll get over it in another twenty-four hours. You—"

He waddled over and held the door open for us.

I walked past him out into the night. He followed me out to the porch. "Come, come, Lam," he said. "Let's shake hands."

"Shake hands with him, Donald," she said.

He pushed out his hand. It was like picking a chunk of cold oatmeal out of a pot. He looked in my eyes, and said, "You're still sore, Lam."

He dropped my hand. "Have it your own way," he said, and waddled back into the house, slamming the door behind him.

Bertha Cool said, "He's a customer, Donald. We can't quarrel with customers."

I didn't say anything.

CHAPTER NINE

THE CAB driver was waiting for us. He held the door open. Bertha Cool said, "Stillwater Apartments," and pulled herself into the cab. I followed, and said, as the cab driver closed the door, "Didn't you want to go to see Sandra?"

"Not just yet," she said.

The cab lurched into motion. I said, "I've got a wild idea."

"How wild?" she asked.

"Awfully wild."

"Let's hear it, Donald."

"A couple of things about this case are screwy. I have a hunch Cunweather is connected with this slot-machine business. He's probably the higher-up. Morgan Birks was contact man. Morgan was given money for a pay-off, and now that information about the pay-off is commencing to come out before the grand jury, it appears that Morgan Birks was making a rake-off of his own. In other words, every time he told the ring they had to pay off a hundred dollars, the pay-off was really only fifty He was giving fifty to the cops, and salting fifty in a safety deposit box."

"There's nothing wild about that idea," she said, groping around in her bag for a cigarette, "and nothing very original. It's been done before—you're probably right at that."

"Wait a minute," I said. "I'm coming to something."

She pulled out her cigarette, and said, "Go ahead and come to it."

"Earlier in the evening Cunweather was confident that Morgan Birks never got to the Perkins Hotel. He seemed to know everything I did at the Perkins Hotel. I played one person at the Perkins Hotel for information. That person was the bell captain. The bell captain must have been one of their gang who was planted there."

She said, "That's sense."

"Then they must have planted the bell captain before I got there."

"That's right."

"And it probably took a little money and preparation so they must have been working on that for a day or two."

"All right."

"But the Perkins Hotel didn't actually figure in the play until Sally Durke went there," I said, "and I was right on her heels. And the bell captain was pretty well established by that time."

"That means they had a good tip-off service," she said.

"It means more than that. How did anyone know Sally Durke was coming to the Perkins Hotel? She didn't have any occasion to meet Morgan Birks until after I'd gone to her and made my play. That was what started her hunting for Morgan."

"Go ahead. What's your idea, Donald?"

I said, "Cunweather knew Birks used the hotel as a place to meet his sweetie. He didn't know who the girl was. He did know Morgan Birks would come there to meet the girl sooner or later. Cunweather is a pretty able citizen. You can gamble he had that hotel sewed up so Birks couldn't get in or out. Yet Birks got in, and he got out."

Mrs. Cool said, "What the hell are you trying to pull, Donald? You say he couldn't get in or get out—and yet he *did* get in and get out. You're the one who's screwy."

"Look here," I said. "Let's figure this thing from a different angle. Notice that they put us in room 620. I tried to get a room across the hall. That's what a detective would ordinarily have done. He'd have wanted a room where he could watch the door of Sally Durke's room. But all of those rooms had been taken. Now that *may* have been an accident. You'd think so if it weren't for the fact that Sally Durke had reserved room 620 for me."

"For *you*, Donald?" she asked.

"Yes."

"How do you figure?"

"She'd telephoned in and reserved two rooms with connecting bath. She had 618 and 620. When she came in, she took 618. Unless there was another bath in connection with that, she took the room without the bath. That left 620 *with the bath* for me. Now that was damned considerate of Sally, no matter how you try to figure it."

"But what makes you think she left it for you?"

"Everything. She wanted me to have the room with the bath because *she wanted me to use the bath.*"

"But you didn't use it. Bleatie was in there."

"Can't you see?" I said. "That's the whole thing. Bleatie was *intended* to be in there. Bleatie isn't Sandra's brother. He's her husband. Bleatie's Morgan Birks!"

She looked at me with cold, hard eyes, and said, "Don't be a God damn ass, Donald."

"Everything points to it." I went on, "We've been dumb not to see it before this."

"Don't you suppose Sandra Birks knows her own brother when she sees him?"

"Of course she does—if she has a brother. But she was in on this play. That explains why Bleatie was always sticking up for Morgan. It explains why he made Sandra kick through with a release of any property that was in the safety deposit boxes. It explains every single fact in the whole case. Sandra Birks wanted a divorce. Morgan Birks was willing to give it to her—probably wanted a divorce just as badly as she did. But she had to serve papers on him. He was a fugitive from justice. Someone had to make the service—someone who could go into court and swear that the service had been made. That's where we came in. We were the fall guys."

"But she met Bleatie at the train, and had this automobile accident and—"

"Look up that automobile accident," I said, "and you'll find that there wasn't any. It was all a frame-up. They hired this doctor to put splints on the man's nose. It was a big heavy nose guard which ran pretty well up to his forehead. Then there was tape to pull his eyes out of shape and twist his mouth. You certainly couldn't see what he looked like with his face all patched up with that nose business.

"That's the only possible explanation to account for the facts. Cunweather was watching the hotel and apparently making a good job of it. He's absolutely certain Morgan Birks never went into that hotel. He wouldn't be mistaken. He was fooled. Dr. Holoman is in on the play. We were taken for a ride. The whole thing was a frame-up. I *thought* that Durke girl was too damned easy. She went directly to the Perkins Hotel and never looked back. The skids were all greased for us. I telephoned Sandra where I was. Sandra and Bleatie insisted on coming up, very much against my wishes. From there on, the play was all blue-printed. Bleatie pretended to work up a blood pressure and have a hemorrhage. Dr. Holoman took him in to the bathroom. As soon as he got in the bathroom, and closed the door to my room, Sally Durke opened the bathroom door of her room. Bleatie changed his clothes, took off his nose bandages, came in, and lay down on the bed. That elaborate combination of splints and tape to protect his broken nose was really a mask to conceal his appearance. The adhesive tape plastered over his forehead and cheekbones pulled his eyes out of shape. Bleatie had black hair that was parted in the middle and combed down on each side, but there was a bald spot on top of his head. Now, no man on earth with thick black hair in front would part it in the middle and comb it down the sides and leave a bald spot staring naked and unadorned from the top of his head. Morgan Birks had black hair and a bald spot. He combed his hair straight back."

Bertha Cool's eyes narrowed. "That would account for them being so worked up when you stayed away so long. They were having a hard time keeping that bathroom business going. But how about the blood on the towels and things?"

"It wasn't blood. It was mercurochrome or some stain the doctor had fixed up to resemble blood. Lord, I don't know all the details. I'm giving you the big play. It *could* have been done that way. Everything fits together when you figure it like that. There's no other way things *do* figure. There's no other way it could have been done.

"Bleatie went into the bathroom, took off his nose business, and became Morgan Birks. He went into 618 and waited until I'd served him. As soon as we went out of 618, he jumped off the bed, went back into the bathroom, changed the parting of his hair, changed back into his bloodstained clothes, had his nose guard taped back into place, and became Bleatie again. Then it was a cinch for him to add the finishing touch. Standing in the bathroom, he was able to impersonate Morgan Birks as calling from 618, and Bleatie as answering from the bathroom. Bleatie's voice was distinguished from Morgan's because it sounded as though Bleatie was talking with a clothespin over his nose. And that bandage business made a perfect disguise. In that way he was able to come to the hotel and leave it right under the noses of the gang that was looking for him. That's the way he's been able to dodge the police. He's been at the place where they least expected him, living in his own apartment with his own little wife. She's covering him up in order to get that divorce. That's why he's so sore at Holoman."

"Being sore at Holoman doesn't fit in," she said. "The doctor must be in on it with him. He must be a confederate."

"Sure, he's in with Birks, but only on this one play. Birks didn't get Holoman. Sandra did. Holoman is Sandra's friend. Morgan and Sandra came to a parting of the ways. Morgan told her about his mistress, and she admitted having a lover. They fixed up the divorce business. They needed a doctor to fix up the disguise. Sandra's lover was called in."

The taxi driver drew up in front of the Stillwater Apartments.

"How much is the meter, Donald, darling?" she asked.

"Four dollars and fifteen cents."

She handed the cab driver a five-dollar bill. "Give me seventy-five cents," she said, "and keep the rest." He gave her a fifty-cent piece and a quarter.

She turned to me. "Donald," she said, "you're a darling. You're the fair-haired boy child. This job takes brains, and you've got them!" She put her arm around my shoulders and said, "Donald, I could love you for this. You figured the thing out, and here is where Bertha Cool goes to town. I'll make a clean-up on this, you darling!—and you owe ninety-five cents on this taxi meter, Donald. I'll take it out of your salary."

She stood on the sidewalk, fished a notebook out of her purse, and marked three dollars and thirty cents in her expense account under taxis. Then she turned the page, and marked down D. L., advance on taxi meter, ninety-five cents.

I said, "Thanks for your praise, Mrs. Cool. Some day I'll try to think of an idea that will cost me an even dollar."

She closed her notebook, dropped it into her purse, smiled at the cab driver, and said to me, "None of your lip, Donald." As soon as the cab driver had pulled away from the curb, she grabbed my arm and swung me around. "All right, Donald, darling, let's go. We'll cash in on this."

"Going to Sandra?" I asked.

"No, no," she said. "To Dr. Holoman. We'll make him jump through hoops."

CHAPTER TEN

IT WAS getting daylight. Somewhere over behind the wall of gray, toneless buildings was a streak of dawn-colored sky. Colorless gray light filtered into the street. Buildings seemed shadowy and unreal, but bulked high against the sky.

We walked three blocks before we found a cruising cab. While Bertha Cool was getting in, I said to the cab driver, "Get us to the nearest place where we can find a telephone directory."

He tried to run us to the Union Depot, but Bertha Cool spotted an all night restaurant and said to me, "Slide back that glass, Donald, dear, and let me talk to that son of a bitch."

I slid back the glass.

"Where the hell do you think *you're* going?" she asked the driver. "Turn around and go back to that restaurant. When I say the *nearest* phone, I mean the nearest."

The driver mumbled something about having to watch for traffic and swung the car. Bertha said to me, "Look under the classified lists, Donald. Find a Holoman who's a doctor. And remember this cab is costing me waiting time—don't take all day."

"I don't think he's a full-fledged doctor yet. He won't have an office. I'll have to call the hospitals. I'll need some nickels."

She sighed, dug four nickels out of her purse and said, "For God's sake, Donald, get some action. I can't charge this as an expense, This is a gamble. I'm using *my* money."

I took the coins, went in and started calling hospitals. The second one was the Shelley Foundation Hospital. The girl said they had an Archie Holoman serving as an interne.

I thanked her, hung up and told the scowling taxi driver to take us to the Shelley Foundation Hospital and climbed back in beside Bertha Cool.

It was a short run, and the cab driver made it fast. Mrs. Cool said, "He probably isn't on duty now, Donald. Get his home address—unless he happens to be living at the hospital. I'll wait here."

I ran up the marble stairs and into the hospital. It was rapidly growing lighter. The freshness of dawn in the air made the interior of the hospital seem steeped with the exudations of sickness and death. A tired-eyed nurse, sitting behind a desk, looked up at me. Daylight streaming through an easterly window, mingled with the lamp light on her face, made it gray and pasty.

"A Dr. Archie Holoman has a position here as interne?" I asked.

"Yes."

"I want very much to see him, please."

"He's on duty. Just a moment, I think I can get him on the telephone. What is your name, please?"

"Lam," I said. "Donald Lam."

"Does he know you?"

"Yes."

The nurse went over and spoke to the switchboard operator. Then after a minute or two motioned to a phone booth, and said, "You can talk with him in there if you wish, Mr. Lam, or here at the desk."

I chose the booth. I knew I had to be careful with my approach. I didn't want him to think I was bluffing. I figured it would be best to let him know I was wise to the play all the way through.

"Donald Lam, Doctor. I wanted to talk to you about exactly what happened when those papers were served on Mr. Birks this afternoon. And I wanted to check your diagnosis on a broken-nose case. I wonder if you'd mind coming down for a moment. Mrs. Cool is here in the cab."

"What's the name?" he asked.

"Lam. Donald Lam. You know, the investigator."

"I'm afraid I don't place you, Mr. Lam."

I said patiently, "You remember when you were patching up Bleatie's broken nose out at Sandra's apartment?"

"I'm quite certain you're mistaken," he said. "You've confused me with someone else. I'm not practicing as yet."

So that was it. He was afraid to have the hospital know he'd been handling any medical work.

"Pardon me," I said. "I guess I made a mistake there. However, Doctor, I'd like to talk with you for a moment. Is it possible for you to come down? We wouldn't talk here," I added hastily, as he hesitated. "Mrs. Cool's outside in the taxicab. We could talk out there."

"I'll come down," he said, "to find out what the devil this is all about."

I thanked him, hung up the receiver, and walked out to stand in the lobby, looking through the plate glass windows into the freshness of early morning. After a few minutes, I heard the elevator descend and turned to greet Dr. Holoman. It wasn't he.

A young man stepped from the elevator, walked across to the nurse's desk. I turned back to look out of the window. After a moment, I heard the sound of low-voiced conversation. The young man walked across to stand just behind me.

I turned.

"You wanted to see me?" he asked.

"No, I'm waiting for Dr. Holoman."

"But I'm Dr. Holoman."

I said, "I guess you're right, Doctor, there's been a mistake. I want Dr. *Archie* Holoman."

"But *I* am Dr. *Archie* Holoman."

I looked him over. He was somewhere in the late twenties, or perhaps had just turned thirty. He was an earnest, sincere-looking chap, with a pallid face, high cheekbones, smoldering black eyes, and dark, wavy hair. I said, "Would you mind stepping out to the taxicab with me? I'd like to have you explain to Mrs. Cool that you're not the Dr. Holoman she's looking for."

I could see he was suspicious. He glanced over at the nurse, then out to where the taxicab was standing at the curb. Then he looked me over, evidently figured he could handle me if he had to, said curtly, "Very well," and accompanied me out to the door of the taxicab. I said, "Mrs. Cool, this is Dr. Holoman, Dr. *Archie* Holoman."

She looked him over and said, "The hell it is!"

After a moment, he said lamely, "I'm pleased to meet you, Mrs. Cool. Was there something I could do?"

"Not a damn thing," she said. "Hop in, Donald."

"Thank you very much, Doctor," I told him.

He looked at me then with the growing conviction that we were both crazy. I hopped into the car. Mrs. Cool gave the driver Sandra's address, and the cab jerked into motion, leaving Dr.

Holoman standing there at the curb looking at us with the expression of a man who has reached for a purse on April First, only to find it jerked out from under his fingers.

"Well," I said, "the plot thickens."

"Thickens, hell," she said. "It's like gravy that's had too much flour dumped in it. It's full of lumps. Are you *sure* that was Dr. Holoman?"

"He said he was, and the hospital said he was."

She fumbled around in her purse, and said, "Donald, I'm out of cigarettes."

I gave her one out of my fast-diminishing store, and took one myself.

We shared the same match. She said, "Damned clever, Donald, my boy, damned clever. They needed an authentic background. They couldn't get a real doctor to do the dirty work, so they stole an interne's identity and background. If we'd ever wanted to check back on Dr. Holoman, we'd have found his record, date, graduation, present location, and all of that. There wasn't one chance in fifty we'd have gone to Dr. Holoman at the hospital."

"That," I said, "brings up the question: Who was the chap masquerading as Dr. Holoman?"

"Her boy friend, probably," she said. "Where there's so much smoke, there's apt to be some fire."

We rode for a while in silence. She turned to me, and said, "Now listen, Donald. Don't be a damn fool about this."

"Meaning what?" I asked.

"You're just about half in love with that Hunter woman."

"Make it two-thirds," I said, "if you're going in for fractions."

"All right. Call it two-thirds. Hell, I don't care. Call it a hundred per cent. She's in a jam. You're going to try and save her. Now don't get excited. Keep your shirt on, and look at the facts. She lied to you about the shooting."

I said, "I'm not certain that she did."

"No," Mrs. Cool observed dryly, "you wouldn't be."

There was another interval of silence.

"You had some plan?" I asked.

"Yes."

"What is it?"

She said, "We'll pin the killing on Bleatie."

"Not so hot," I objected. "We've just established that there isn't any Bleatie."

"That makes it swell," she said. "It gives the police a hard nut to crack. The way the thing stands now, there were two persons—Bleatie and Morgan Birks. We are the only outsiders who know Morgan Birks and Bleatie were the same people. Morgan Birks is dead. Therefore Bleatie is dead too. No one knows Bleatie is dead. They can't ever prove it because they can't ever find his body. We pin everything on Bleatie—if she pays us enough.

"Now, you walk in there and spill what you know, and everyone says, 'That's right. Clever of the boy, but we were right on the verge of reasoning it out ourselves. Another half hour and we'd have had it.' But we go in there and start asking where Bleatie is, and pretty quick some damn flatfoot gets the idea Bleatie's guilty of murder. Play it that way and you've got something."

"But how could any flatfoot figure Bleatie'd kill anyone when Alma Hunter admits she raised the gun and pulled the trigger?"

"That's where *our* ingenuity comes in," she said. "If Sandra wants us to clear Alma Hunter of the charge, and I think she does, and pays enough for it, and I hope she will, we drag

Bleatie into it by the ears. Alma Hunter was hysterical. She was excited. She doesn't *know* what happened. She heard a shot, and she thought it came from the gun she was holding in her hand. Really it didn't. It was fired by Bleatie, who was in the room."

"What was he doing in her room?" I asked.

"Looking at her etchings."

"And Alma didn't know he was there?"

"No."

"And Alma didn't shoot at all?"

"No, of course not."

"But suppose it's her gun that's on the floor?"

"No, it wasn't her gun. She screamed, dropped her gun and ran. Bleatie picked up her gun, left the gun with which the killing had been done, and walked out into the night."

"That," I said, "is a pretty tall order."

"We can make it sound plausible."

"I don't think I like your way," I said. "I think I like mine. What's more, the police won't like yours."

"The police have hands, ears, eyes, legs, noses, and mouths just the same as we do. They can gather the facts and draw conclusions just the same as we can. It isn't up to us to prove that girl innocent. It's up to the police to show that she's guilty. If we can account for the circumstances by some other explanation which doesn't leave any loose threads dangling, that's all we need to offer to a jury. That's the law."

"Well," I said, "that's not an exact statement of the law, but it's close enough."

"Now then," she demanded, "do you want to get Alma Hunter out of this or not?"

"Yes."

"All right then. Keep your mouth shut, and let Auntie Bertha do the talking."

The cab pulled up in front of Sandra's apartment house. A police guard was stationed in the lobby. Apparently the few early morning stragglers had no inkling of what had happened. There was no outward indication of a homicide.

Bertha Cool paid off the cab and barged up to the apartment house. The officer said, "Just a moment. Do you live here?"

"No."

"Where are you going?"

"To call on Sandra Birks."

"What's your name?"

"Bertha Cool, head of the Cool Detective Agency. This is one of my operatives."

"What do you want?"

"To see Sandra Birks."

"What do you want to see her about?"

"I don't know. She wants to see me. What's the matter? Is she under arrest?"

"No, not under arrest."

"It's her apartment, isn't it?"

"Oh, go on up," he said.

"Thanks. I intend to," Mrs. Cool announced.

I tried to be polite about the door, but she beat me to it, grabbed the knob and flung the heavy door back as though it had been made of cardboard. She strode on in, and I came along in her wake. We took the elevator to the fourth floor. Sandra Birks flung open the door as I tapped gently on the panels.

"It took you long enough to get here."

Bertha Cool said, "We didn't want to run into the police."

"There's a guard downstairs."

"I know."

"Did he try to stop you?"

"Yes."

"How did you get by?"

"Walked by."

"You told him you were a detective?"

"Yes."

"Would he let anyone in who wasn't a detective?"

"How the hell do I know, dearie? He's a cop. You can't tell what a cop will do."

Sandra bit her lip and frowned. "I'm expecting a young man—a friend of ours—I wonder if they'll take him into custody—"

"Better call him up and head him off," I said.

"I think they have my line tapped. I think they're leaving me here as bait for a trap."

"What sort of a trap?"

"I don't know."

Bertha Cool said, "Let's take a look in the bedroom, then we'll talk."

Sandra Birks opened the bedroom door. A chalked outline on the carpet showed where the body had lain. A section had been sawed from the door, a small square piece cut out of the wood.

"What's that?" Bertha Cool wanted to know. "Where the bullet was imbedded?"

"Yes."

"Are they sure the bullet came from that gun?"

"That's what they're going to find out."

Bertha Cool said, "Where did she get the gun?"

"That's what I can't understand. I'm absolutely certain she didn't have one yesterday morning."

Bertha Cool looked at me. Her eyes were steady, thoughtful, and filled with rebuke.

"Where's your brother?" she asked.

Sandra Birks shifted her eyes. "I'm sure I don't know."

"Where was he when the shooting occurred?"

"In his room, I guess. He was supposed to be there."

"Where is he now?"

"I don't know."

"Had his bed been slept in?"

"No, he evidently hadn't retired."

"Rather late for him to be up, wasn't it?" Mrs. Cool asked.

"I don't know," Sandra said with a flare of temper. "I was out myself. Of course, if I'd known my husband was going to be shot, I might have planned the evening differently. But no one told me; therefore, I didn't sit by my brother's bedside to see what time he retired or what his plans were."

"Anything else?" Mrs. Cool asked.

"What do you mean?"

"Is there anything else you want to say?"

"Why?"

"Because," Bertha Cool said calmly, "it's costing you money to talk to me. If you want to spend your money trying to stand between your brother and the consequences of his act, it's all right with me. I'll listen as long as you want to talk, dearie."

Sandra had been talking with that swift, vehement articulation which a woman of her type uses when she's putting on a counter offensive, trying to cover something up. Now her eyes showed puzzled surprise. "What do you mean, standing between him and the consequences of his act?"

Bertha Cool said, "You know what I mean, dearie. Your brother murdered your husband," and then, as Sandra Birks started to say something, she turned to me and said, "Come on, Donald, let's take a look through the other rooms. I suppose the police have messed things up like hell, but we'll look around anyway."

She started walking before she was finished talking. Her huge figure moved slowly and majestically through the door, and I followed along behind.

Sandra Birks was standing in the middle of the floor, her eyes clouded with thought.

"You talked with Bleatie in the other bedroom, Donald?" Bertha Cool asked.

"Yes."

"Show me where it is."

I detoured around her and took the lead. Sandra Birks remained in the bedroom with the twin beds. When I had opened the door to Bleatie's room, Bertha Cool said, "Not that I give a good God damn about what's in here, Donald, my love, I'm just giving her time to realize the possibilities of the situation."

"You think she wants to protect Alma Hunter?" I asked.

"Of course, otherwise why did she want to have us on the job?"

"Perhaps," I said, "she's already said too much to the police. *They* must have asked about her brother."

"Well, let's hope it's nothing she can't lie out of afterwards," Bertha Cool said. "She doesn't impress me as beung a particularly wide-open type. She's secretive and furtive as hell. You ask her what the weather is, and she'll find some way of avoiding the subject very tactfully, stopping just short of telling you whether it's raining or sunny, hot or cold—so this is Bleatie's room. Well, let's take a look around."

Bertha Cool started opening bureau drawers, making a

quick mental inventory of the contents, and closing them again. Suddenly she swooped down on the interior of a drawer, and pulled out something bulky. "Now then," she said, "what the hell is this?"

"Looks like a cloth life preserver," I said.

"Straps on the back," she mused. "I have it, Donald. There was something wrong about Bleatie's figure. Remember that watermelon stomach he had—not watermelon exactly, sort of a cantaloupe stomach?

"Well, Morgan Birks didn't. Morgan Birks was slender. He had a dimple where his stomach should have been. This was the gadget Morgan Birks put on when he wanted to become Bleatie."

I looked it over. That's what it was, all right.

Bertha Cool calmly rolled it up and said, "See if you can find me a newspaper somewhere, Donald, my love. We'll just take this God damn thing away with us. It doesn't need to figure in the case at all."

There was no newspaper there in the room. I walked out into the living room and met Sandra Birks coming from the other bedroom. "Where's Mrs. Cool?" she asked.

I indicated the bedroom, and Sandra walked on past me. There was a newspaper on the table, lying on top of the pile of magazines. I picked it up, spread it out so it was flat on the table and then waited for a couple of minutes before I walked back to the bedroom and said, "I'll fix it."

Bertha Cool and Sandra were facing each other. I heard Mrs. Cool say, "Don't tell me anything, dearie, until you've had a chance to think it all out. You're all nervous and upset. Keep your trap closed until you've thought it out *carefully*, and then we'll talk about dough."

"I've thought it out," Sandra said.

Mrs. Cool handed me the cloth padding, and said, "Wrap it up, Donald. Tie it good and tight, and then bring it back."

I took plenty of time wrapping the bundle. I made a good job of it. I found some string in a drawer in the kitchenette and put in lots of knots. I'd just finished tying it when imperative knuckles banged on the door and a voice said, "Open up."

I left the package on the table, put my hat over it, and called to Sandra Birks, "There's someone at the door."

She walked from Bleatie's room to the door of the apartment. The man on the outside was pounding on the panels again before she had the door open.

Two plain-clothes men pushed into the room. One said, "Okay, sister, the jig's up."

"What do you mean?" she asked.

"The gun that killed Morgan Birks was the gun that killed Johnny Meyer, and Johnny Meyer, just in care you don't know it, was the Kansas City detective who had been working on the organized rackets. He was to go before the grand jury and blow the lid off. He never got there. He was last seen alive with a good-looking frail. He was found the next morning with three slugs in his chest. The K. C. police broadcast photomicrographs of the bullets, and warned all police officers to be on the lookout for the gun.

"Now then, sister, suppose *you* start talking."

Sandra Birks stood very straight, very white, and very frightened.

Bertha Cool came out from Bleatie's bedroom. The second plain-clothes man said to Sandra, "Who are these people?"

"We're detectives," Bertha Cool said.

"You're *what?*"

"Detectives."

The man laughed.

Bertha Cool said, "Private detectives, investigating this thing at Mrs. Birks' request."

"Get out," the officer ordered.

Bertha Cool settled herself complacently in a chair. "Throw me out," she invited.

I glanced significantly at my hat and the newspaper package on the table. "I'll leave," I said.

Bertha Cool caught my eye as I picked up my hat and the newspaper-wrapped package.

"I'm within my rights," she said. "If you want to arrest Mrs. Birks, go ahead. If you want to talk with her, go ahead. But I'm here, and I'm going to stay here."

"You just think you're going to stay here," the officer roared, pushing toward her belligerently.

Sandra Birks silently held the door open for me. As the two officers converged on Bertha Cool, I slipped out into the corridor. I didn't dare wait for the elevator. I sprinted for the stairs, and went down them two at a time. I slowed down halfway down the last flight, walked casually across the lobby as though I had a bundle of laundry with me, and gained the sidewalk. The police car was parked in front of the place.

An attendant was commencing to move automobiles out of the apartment house garage and park them at the curb. I picked a prosperous-looking machine on the theory that the owner would be sleeping late, climbed in and sat down, leaving the package on the seat beside me.

Bertha Cool came marching majestically out of the apartment house, looked up and down the street, and then started toward the corner. She didn't see me in the automobile as she walked past. I let her go. After she'd walked another fifty feet I could pick her up in the rear-view mirror of the automobile. Apparently she was puzzled by my complete disappearance. She stopped twice before she got to the corner, looking around inquiringly. At the corner, she turned left. I couldn't tell whether she had headed for the better-traveled streets, looking for a taxicab, or whether she was still looking for me. I didn't dare to turn around. I kept slouched in the seat, glancing in the rear-view mirror occasionally, but keeping my attention focused on the entrance of the apartment house.

After a while the two plain-clothes officers came out. Sandra Birks wasn't with them. They stood for a moment talking. Then they got in the car and drove away.

I picked up my newspaper package, slid out of the automobile, and walked rapidly toward the apartment house. A big refuse can had been dragged out by the janitor and was placed near the curb. I opened the lid and dropped my package into the can, replaced the lid, and went directly to Sandra Birks' apartment. She didn't open the door until I'd knocked twice. She hadn't been crying, but her eyes were dark and her cheeks seemed to be all caved in. Her mouth looked drawn and hard. She said, "You!"

I slipped in through the door, closed it behind me and snapped the bolt.

"The package," she asked. "How about it? Did you get rid of it?"

I nodded.

She said, "You shouldn't have come back here."

"I had to talk with you," I said.

She put her hand on my shoulder. "Oh, I'm so frightened,"

she said. "I don't know what it means. Do you suppose that Morgan—that Alma—"

I slipped my arm around her waist and said, "Take it easy, Sandra."

That arm seemed to be the signal she was waiting for. She insinuated her body up close to mine. Her eyes looked into mine. "Donald," she said, "you must help me."

And then she kissed me.

She may have had other things on her mind. Probably there was plenty to worry her, but it didn't interfere with that kiss. There was nothing sisterly or platonic about it.

After a moment she held her head back so she could look into my eyes. "Donald," she said, "I'm depending on you." Then before I had a chance to say anything, she said, "Oh, Donald, you're such a *dear*. It's such a comfort to me, knowing that I have you to depend on."

"Hadn't we," I suggested, "better get *my* mind on *our* work?"

"Oh, Donald, you *will* help me, won't you?"

"What do you suppose I came back for?" I asked.

She was smoothing my hair back with the tips of her fingers. "I feel so much better already," she said. "I feel that I can trust you, Donald. I've felt that way from the first. I'd do anything for you, Donald. There's something about you that—"

"I want some money," I said.

She stopped. "You want what?"

"Money."

"What do you mean money?"

"Currency," I said. "Lots of it."

"Why Donald, I gave Mrs. Cool a retainer."

"Unfortunately," I said, "Mrs. Cool hasn't joined any of the

Share-the-Wealth movements— At any rate, not as we go to press."

"But you're working for her, aren't you?"

"I thought you wanted me to work for *you*," I said. "Perhaps I misunderstood you."

"But, Donald, *she's* working for me, and you're working for her."

"All right," I said. "Have it your own way."

She slowly pushed herself back so that the warmth of her body was no longer perceptible through my clothes. "Donald," she said, "I don't understand you."

"All right," I said. "I thought perhaps you would. It's my mistake. I'll go hunt up Bertha Cool."

"How much money would you want?" she asked.

"Lots of it."

"How much?"

"When you hear how much," I said, "it's going to knock the props out from under you."

"But why do you want it?"

"For expenses."

"What are you going to do?"

"I'm going to take the rap," I said.

"Donald, tell me what you mean."

I said, "Bertha Cool's got funny ideas. She thinks she can use Bleatie as a red herring and blame this on him simply because Bleatie can't be found. She might have done just that if it had been a simple bedroom killing. The way the cards stack up now, it can't be done. A Kansas City police officer was killed. You know how cops feel about people who shoot police officers. They don't like it."

"What do you mean, you're going to take the rap, Donald?"

she asked, her eyes shrewd and calculating as she searched my face.

"I mean I'm going the whole hog," I said. "I'm going to give you both an out. I'm going to say I shot him, but I've got to do it in my way."

"But, Donald, they'll hang you," she said.

"They won't hang me."

"But, Donald, you can't. You wouldn't be willing to. You couldn't be—"

"We can either waste time arguing about it," I said, "or we can do something about it. Those cops didn't take you into custody because they decided they didn't have enough on you, and a smart lawyer could get you loose. So they figured they'd give you plenty of rope and see just how you'd go about hanging yourself. They also wanted to see what other fish would get drawn into the net. As soon as they get back and report to police headquarters they'll have this apartment sewed up so tight not even a cockroach could get out without being picked up and shadowed and classified. Do you want to wait for that?"

"Of course I don't."

"I don't either. I want to get out before that happens. That means just about now."

I started for the door.

"How much do you want, Donald?"

"Three thousand dollars."

"Three what?" she cried.

"Thousand," I said. "Three grand. I want it now."

"Donald, you talk as though you were crazy."

"You act as though you were," I said. "This is your only out. I'm giving it to you. Do you want it, or don't you?"

"How do I know I can trust you?" she asked.

I wiped lipstick off my lips and said, "You don't know."

"I've been betrayed lots of times by men whom I've trusted."

"How much did Morgan leave in those safety deposit boxes?" I asked.

"He didn't have any."

"They were in your name. It won't be long until the police sew those up too."

She laughed then, and said, "Do I look as though I was born yesterday?"

"I suppose," I observed, "you went out and stripped the boxes, and thought you were being smart. By the time the prosecuting attorney gets finished with that, it'll make a swell motive for murder."

I could see startled realization in her eyes.

"And if you happen to have that money on you," I said, "you're just crazy, because every move you make from now on is going to be shadowed. Sooner or later the police are going to take you down to jail and a great big broad-hipped matron is going to take all your nice clothes off and search your pretty little body. While that's going on, detectives will be searching the apartment. What do you think of that?"

"Donald, they wouldn't?"

"They're going to."

She said, "It's in a money belt on me."

"How much?" I asked.

"Lots."

I said, "You don't dare to ditch it all, Sandra. You'd better leave some money, a hundred or two, in the money belt so they won't realize you've slipped one over on them. As far as the rest is concerned, you can do either one of two things. You can either trust it to me, knowing that I may go south with it; or you can split it up in a lot of letters, address those letters to yourself at general delivery, and drop them in the mail chute. You'd better do something quick."

It took her about five seconds to make up her mind. During those five seconds she stood staring at me, her head slightly on one side. I stood still. She looked at me and I met her look. Then she unsnapped buttons at the side of her skirt, slipped it down and fumbled with buckles—it wasn't exactly a money belt. It was a money corset. She handed it to me. I couldn't get it around me. I loosened my belt, shoved it down along my back, and pinched my belt tight.

"God knows why I'm doing this," she said. "I'm putting myself absolutely in your power. I'm stripping myself of everything."

I said, "Just one thing—Give Alma a square deal and I'll give you a square deal. I'm doing this for her."

"Not for me?" she asked, pushing out her lips in a little pout.

"No," I said. "For Alma."

"Oh, Donald, I thought it was because you—"

"Well, think again," I said, and stepped out into the corridor, pulling the door shut behind me.

I'd got as far as the head of the stairs when she opened the door and screamed, "Donald, come back here!"

I went down the stairs in a rush. I heard her scream and run after me. I must have beat her to the lobby by a matter of seconds. I started through the door. A car was parked in front of the place with two men seated in it. They weren't the two plainclothes men who had been there earlier. The way in which they looked up as I came out showed what they were.

I pretended not to see them, crossed to an automobile, got in, and stepped on the starter, leaning forward as I did so, so that my head was lowered almost below the line of the windows.

She came dashing out to the street, looking up and down, her face showing puzzled bewilderment as she saw I was nowhere in sight. She started to run toward the corner. The officers exchanged glances. One of them climbed leisurely from the car. "Looking for something?" he asked.

She turned to look at him—and knew.

"I thought I heard someone yell fire," she said. "—Is there a fire?"

The officer said, "You're dreaming, sister."

To my surprise the ignition wasn't locked. The motor of the car I was in throbbed to life.

I straightened up. She caught sight of me then, and stood there with the eyes of the officer on her, powerless to do anything.

I'll hand it to her. She played the one card that would have got her by. Her lips quivered, and she said, "I'm awfully n-n-nervous this morning. My husband was m-m-murdered."

I saw tension go out of the officer's frame. "That," he said sympathetically, "is too bad. May I see you up to your apartment?"

I drove away.

CHAPTER ELEVEN

I REGISTERED at the Perkins Hotel as Rinton C. Watson of Klamath Falls, Oregon. I got a room with a bath and asked the bellboy to have the captain step up to the room for a minute.

The captain had that smirk of simulated deference which characterizes pimps, panderers and procurers the world over. He thought he knew what I wanted before I'd said a word. "You aren't the one I want," I said.

"I can do anything for you that any of the others can."

"No, it's not that. I wanted to see a man, an old friend."

"What was his name?"

"I think," I said, "it's been changed."

He laughed. "Tell me what it was, and I may know it."

"You would if I told you," I observed, letting him see suspicion in my eyes.

He quit laughing. "There are three of us on duty," he said.

"Live here in the hotel?" I asked.

"I do. I have a room down in the basement. The others live out."

"This man," I said, "is about twenty-five, with very thick black hair. It comes down low in the center of his forehead. He has a short, stubby nose and slate-colored eyes."

"Where'd you know him?" he asked.

I deliberated for a while before I said, "Kansas City."

The answer registered. The bell captain made a gesture of co-operation. "That's Jerry Wegley. He comes on duty at four this afternoon and works until midnight."

"Wegley," I mused.

"That the name you knew him under?" the captain asked curiously.

I hesitated perceptibly before saying, "Yes."

"I see."

"Where could I reach him?"

"Here, after four o'clock."

"I mean now."

"I might find out his address—perhaps you'd like to talk with him over the telephone."

"I'd have to see him," I said. "*I* was going under another name when he knew me."

"I'll see what I can do."

"Do that," I said, and locked the door as he went out. I took the money corset out of my belt and started taking out fifties and hundreds. There was eight thousand four hundred and fifty dollars in all. I put the bills in four rolls, distributed them in my trousers pockets, and rolled the corset-belt into a compact bundle.

The bellboy came back. "It's Brinmore Rooms," he said. "If Jerry isn't glad to see you, don't tell him where you got the information."

I gave him a fifty-dollar bill. "Could you," I asked, "bring me forty-five dollars in return for this?"

His face broke into a cheerful grin. "Surest thing you know," he said. "I'll be back with the forty-five in five minutes."

"Bring me a newspaper, too," I told him.

When he returned with the forty-five dollars and the newspaper, I wrapped up the corset-belt and walked out of the hotel. I went to the Union Depot, sat down on one of the benches for a few minutes, then got up and walked away, leaving the newspaper-wrapped parcel on the seat.

From the branch post office I purchased a stamped envelope and a special delivery stamp. I addressed the envelope to Jerry Wegley, Brinmore Rooms, tore a page of newspaper into strips, folded some of the strips into the envelope, sealed it, and took a taxicab to the Brinmore Rooms.

The Brinmore Rooms consisted of a door on the street level, a flight of stairs, a little counter with a call bell, a register, and a fly-specked pasteboard placard with the words *"Ring for Manager"* printed on it.

I rang.

When nothing happened, I rang again. After another ten seconds, a thin-faced woman with a gold-toothed smile came out to see what I wanted.

"Special delivery letter for Jerry Wegley," I said. "You want to take it in to him?"

"No, he's in 18, straight down the hall," she said shortly, folding her lips back down over her gold teeth and slamming the door of her room behind her as she turned back.

I went on down to 18, knocked three times gently on the door, and got no action. I tried to insert a knife blade along the side of the lock, and decided after five minutes that I was a failure as a burglar. I walked back down the threadbare carpet to the counter with its bell and register, lifted up the hinged gate in the counter, and looked around on the inside. There were a half dozen bundles of laundry, three or four magazines, and a pasteboard suitcase. I kept looking around and finally found what I wanted, a nail with a big heavy wire loop hanging on it. A chain hung from the loop, and the key dangled at the end of the chain. I took care to keep the chain from jingling against the wire as I took the key and walked back down the hall.

The passkey opened room 18 without any difficulty.

The bird had flown the coop.

There was some dirty underwear on the floor of the closet, a sock with a hole in the big toe, a rusty safety razor blade, and the stub of a lead pencil.

The bureau drawers yielded nothing but a frayed necktie which had begun to pull apart in the center, an empty gin bottle and a crumpled cigarette package. The bed hadn't been slept in since it had last been made, although the sheets and pillow cases looked about ready for the laundry.

The place was dingy, smelly, dejected, and deserted. The mirror over the cheap pine bureau threw back a faded, distorted reflection of my face.

I went back to the closet and looked the underwear over for laundry marks. I found an old X-B391. It was pretty well faded. The same number had been written more recently and in a different handwriting on the waistband of the shorts.

I made a note of the number, left the room, locked the door, and paused long enough in front of the counter at the head of the stairs to slide the wire hoop down under the counter where it would look as though it had fallen off the nail.

Jerry Wegley had the last laugh. I'd paid him twenty-five dollars to slip me a gun which was hotter than a stovelid. Wegley went on duty at four o'clock in the afternoon and was off at midnight. He probably went to bed as a rule around two or three o'clock in the morning. This time he hadn't gone to bed.

Had it been because he'd learned what had been done with the gun he'd passed off on me?

I didn't know, and had no immediate way of finding out.

I waited on the street until a cruising cab came along, and went out to the airport. An aviator who made a specialty of chartering planes to bridal couples agreed to take me to Yuma, Arizona, and seemed surprised that I was making the trip alone.

Once in Yuma, I followed a plan of operation which I had rehearsed in my own mind so many times that it made me feel I was playing a part in a play.

I went to the First National Bank, went to the window marked "New Accounts," and said, "My name is Peter B. Smith. I'm looking for some investments."

"What sort of investments, Mr. Smith?"

"Anything that I can turn to quick advantage and make a profit."

The assistant cashier smiled. "A lot of people are looking for these same things, Mr. Smith."

"Exactly," I said. "I don't expect you to help me look, but if I find something, I'd appreciate having your reactions."

"You wish to open an account?"

"Yes."

I took two thousand dollars in cash from my pocket.

"Where're you going to live, Mr. Smith?" he asked.

"I haven't got located yet."

"You came from the East?"

"No, from California."

"Just got in?"

"Yes."

"Did you have a business in California?"

"Just sharpshooting," I said. "But I think California's just about reached the maximum of its growth. Arizona has a long way to go."

That was all the reference I needed. He made out a deposit slip, gave me a withdrawal card to sign, counted the two thousand dollars, and entered the amount in a deposit book. "Do you," he asked, "want a flat checkbook or a pocket checkbook?"

"Pocket."

He fitted a block of blank checks into an imitation leather folder stamped with the name of the bank, and handed it to me. I put it in my pocket, shook hands, and walked out.

I went to the Bank of Commerce, hunted up the new-account man, gave the name of Peter B. Smith, shook hands, told him the same thing, and deposited two thousand dollars. I also rented a safety deposit box and put most of the balance of Sandra Birks' money in there.

It was late afternoon by the time I'd secured a room, paid a month's rent in advance, and explained to the landlady that my baggage would be along later.

I walked around town, sizing up the automobile agencies. I picked the one which looked as though it was doing the largest business, walked in, and asked to be shown a light sedan for immediate delivery. I told the salesman I was thoroughly familiar with the performance of the car, that what I wanted was an immediate delivery. I wanted a car that could start out and go. I'd prefer a demonstrator to a new car. He said he had a demonstrator he could have ready for the road in thirty minutes. I told him I'd be back. He asked if I wanted to buy it on contract, and I said no, I'd pay for it in cash. I whipped the checkbook from my pocket, asked the total amount that would be due, and wrote a check for one thousand six hundred and seventy-two dollars.

I signed the check and said, "This is my first day in Yuma. I am going to be in business here. You don't know of any good investments, do you?"

"What sort of investments?"

"Things where a man can put in a little money, figure on a quick turnover, and a large profit with no risk."

It spoke volumes for his credulity that he stopped and gave the matter frowning concentration for several seconds before he shook his head slowly. "No, I don't know of anything like that right now, but I'll keep you in mind, Mr. Smith. Where are you going to be staying?"

I made a show of trying to recall the address, said, "I have rather a poor memory at times," and fished the rent receipt from my wallet. I held it so he could see the name of the apartment house. "Oh yes," he said, "I know the place. Well, I'll keep in touch with you, Mr. Smith."

"Do that," I said. "I'll be back in half an hour, and I want to be ready to roll."

I went out to a restaurant, ordered the biggest steak on the menu, and polished it off with mince pie à la mode. I went back to the automobile agency to pick up the car. They had pinned my check to the top of a pile of papers.

"You'll have to sign your name here two or three times," the salesman said.

I noticed that someone had written in indelible pencil in the upper left-hand corner of my check, the word "Okay," followed by the initials "GEC." I signed the name Peter B. Smith two or three times, shook hands all around, climbed in the car, and drove out. I went directly to the First National Bank. It lacked about fifteen minutes of closing time. I went to the counter and drew a sight draft on H. C. Helmingford for five thousand six hundred and ninety-two dollars and fifty cents. I drew a counter check for one thousand eight hundred dollars. I went to the cashier's window and said, "I'm Peter Smith. I opened an account here today. I was looking for some investments. I have found one which is going to require immediate cash. I have here a sight draft drawn on H. C. Helmingford. I want this presented to him through the Security National Bank of Los Angeles. It will be honored immediately on presentation. I want it rushed."

He took the draft and said, "Just a minute, Mr. Smith—"

"It isn't necessary," I said. "I don't want you to give me any credit on this. Simply handle it as a collection. Have your Los Angeles correspondent wire back at my expense."

He gave me a receipt for the draft. "And you wanted some cash?" he asked.

"Yes," I said, and handed him the counter check for eighteen hundred dollars, looking at my watch as I did so.

He said, "Just a minute," stepped back to the bookkeeping department to verify the balance and my signature. He hesitated for a moment, then came back and asked, "How do you want this, Mr. Smith?"

"In hundreds," I said.

He gave me the money. I thanked him, drove over to the Bank of Commerce, got into my safety deposit vault, and put the eighteen hundred dollars in with the other money in there. Then I climbed in the car, drove out of town and crossed the bridge over the Colorado River into California. I parked the car for about half an hour, sitting there smoking and letting my dinner digest. Then I started the motor and drove on the few yards that brought me to the California quarantine station over on the right-hand side of the road.

Under the guise of maintaining an agricultural inspection, the California authorities stop every car, search it, unpack baggage, fumigate blankets, ask questions, and inconvenience the motorists as much as possible.

I swung in close to the checking station. A man came out to look me over. I yelled at him, taking care to run the words all together so that he couldn't hear anything except the jumble of sound as I stepped on the gas. He signaled for me to pull into the unloading platform, and I gave the car everything it had.

A couple of hundred yards down the road, my rear-view mirror showed me that a motorcycle officer was kicking the prop out from under his wheels.

I started traveling.

The motorcycle officer came roaring out from the checking station and my car started going places. I heard the siren swell into noise behind me, and let it get close enough so the sound of it helped clear traffic ahead. The officer didn't reach for his gun until after we'd got pretty well into the drifting sand hills. When I saw he was getting ready to shoot, I pulled over to the side and stopped.

The officer wasn't taking any chances on me. He came up alongside with the gun pushed out in front. "Stick 'em up," he said.

I stuck 'em up.

"What the hell's the idea?"

"What idea?"

"Don't pull that line with me."

"Okay," I said, "you've got me. This is a new car. I just bought it in Yuma. I wanted to find out how fast it would go. What does the judge soak me, a dollar a mile over the legal limit?"

"Why didn't you stop in at the quarantine station?"

"I did. The man motioned for me to go on."

"The hell he did. He motioned for you to pull in and stop."

"I misunderstood him," I said.

"You bought this car in Yuma, eh? Where?"

I told him.

"When?"

I told him.

"Turn around," he said. "We're going back."

"Back where?"

"Back to the checking station."

"Like hell we are. I've got business in El Centro."

"You're under arrest."

"All right, then, take me before the nearest and most accessible magistrate."

"How'd you pay for this car?" he asked.

"With a check."

"Ever hear anything about the penalty for issuing bum checks?" he asked.

"No," I said.

He said, "Well, buddy, you're going right back across the bridge into Yuma. The man that sold you this car wants you to answer some questions about that check. You thought you were being pretty cute, but you were just about fifteen minutes too early. They managed to get the check down to the bank before it closed."

"Well, what of it?"

He grinned. "They'll tell you about that when you get back there."

"Back where?"

"Back to Yuma."

"For what?"

"For issuing a bum check, for obtaining property under false pretenses, and probably a couple of other charges."

"I'm not going back to Yuma," I said.

"I think you are."

I reached down and twisted the ignition key. "I know my rights," I said. "I'm in California. You can't take me back across into Arizona without extradition."

"Oh," he said. "Like that, is it?"

"If you want to make it that way."

He nodded. "All right, brother. You want to go to El Centro. Go ahead. We're going there. Keep within the legal limit. I'll be right behind you. Forty-five's the legal limit. I'll allow you fifty. At fifty-one I start shooting out your tires. Do you get me?"

"You can't arrest me without a warrant," I said.

"That's what you think. Get out. I'm going to frisk you."

I sat tight behind the wheel. He put one foot on the running board, shot his left hand out and hooked his fingers in the collar of my shirt. "Come on out," he said, holding the gun menacingly in his right hand.

I came out.

He patted me, looking for weapons, then looked through the car.

"Remember," he said, "both hands on the wheel. No funny stuff. If you want to be extradited, you'll sure as hell be extradited."

"I don't like your manner," I said, "and I resent this high-handed invasion of my rights. I—"

"Get started," he interrupted.

I got started. We drove into El Centro, and he took me to the sheriff's office. I was left in charge of a deputy while the officer and the sheriff did some talking. Then I heard them telephoning. After that, I was taken down to the jail. The sheriff said, "Listen, Smith, you're a nice looking chap. You're not gaining anything by pulling a stunt like this. Why don't you go back and face the music. You may be able to square it."

I said, "I'm not talking."

"All right," he warned, "if you want to be smart."

"I want to be smart," I said.

They put me in a tank with four or five other prisoners. I didn't do any talking. When supper was served, I didn't do any eating. Shortly after supper, the sheriff came back again and asked me if I'd waive extradition. I told him to go to hell and he went out.

I stayed in the tank for two days. I ate some of the grub. It wasn't too bad. The heat was awful. I didn't have a newspaper and didn't know what was going on in the world. They took me out of the tank and put me in a cell by myself. I had no one to talk to.

On the third day, a big man with a black sombrero came in with the sheriff. He said to me, "You Peter B. Smith?"

"Yes."

"I'm from Yuma," he said. "You're going back with me."

"Not without extradition."

"I have extradition."

"Well, I refuse to honor it. I'm going to stay right here."

He grinned.

I gripped the side of the cot and raised my voice. "I'm going to stay right here!"

The big man sighed. "Listen," he said, "it's too God damn hot for strenuous exercise. For Christ's sake, come on out and get in that car."

I yelled at him, "I'm going to stay right here!"

He shoved me around. The Arizona officer snapped handcuffs on my wrists. I refused to talk, and they hauled me out of the jail and into the car.

The big man put on a leg iron. "You asked for this," he said, mopping perspiration from his forehead. "Why can't you be reasonable? Don't you know it's hot?"

"You're going to regret this as long as you live," I said. "I haven't committed any crime and you can't pin one on me. I'll—"

"Forget it. Shut up," he interrupted. "I've got a hot drive across the desert ahead of me, and I don't want to hear the sound of your voice."

"You won't," I said, and sat back against the cushions.

We drove through the shimmering heat of the desert. The horizon twisted and danced in the rays of a blistering sun. The air was so hot it cooked my eyes in their sockets as boiling water boils an egg in its shell. The tires seemed to stick to the road, snarling a steady whine of sticky protest.

"You *would* come at the hottest time of the day," I said.

"Shut up."

I kept quiet.

We drove into Yuma and went to the courthouse. The deputy district attorney said, "You made these people go to a lot of trouble, Smith. Where do you think it's going to get you?"

"They didn't need to go to any trouble," I said. "If they think they've had trouble so far, wait until you see what they get."

"What are they going to get?"

"I'm going to sue them for malicious prosecution, false arrest, and defamation of character."

He yawned and said, "Don't pull that gag. You make me laugh. If it had been a new car, the situation would have been different. As it is, it's a demonstrator. You've given it a few miles' run. It hasn't hurt the car any. But you made them go to the expense of extraditing you. That's going to hurt."

"Why the hell didn't they cash the check I gave them?" I asked.

He laughed and said, "Because you'd been down to the bank and drawn all the money out."

"Nuts," I said. "That was the other bank."

"What do you mean, the other bank?"

"You know what I mean."

"You're damn right I know what you mean. It's the old flim-flam game. You went down and handed out a line of soap. You deposited two thousand dollars in the bank. You left the check, knowing damn well they'd take steps to find out whether the check was good, but they wouldn't cash it until you'd signed the papers and driven out with the car. You figured on getting the car delivered just a few minutes before closing time, beating it down to the bank and drawing out everything except two hundred dollars. You figured you'd have eighteen hours' start before anyone found out the check wasn't any good. But you beat your own time a little, and the automobile agency showed up at the bank about five minutes after you'd left with the money. They deposit every night just before closing time."

I stared at him, letting my eyes get big and my jaw sag. "For God's sake," I said. "Do you mean they tried to cash my check at the First National?"

"Why not? That's the bank it was given on."

"No it wasn't," I said. "That check was issued on the Bank of Commerce."

He showed me the check, marked with the telltale "NSF" in red ink. I said, "Well, then, I drew the eighteen hundred out of the Bank of Commerce."

"Why all the talk about the Bank of Commerce?"

"Because I have an account there."

"The hell you do."

"Yes."

"You don't have anything to prove it."

"I was going to take a long night ride," I said. "I didn't want to have my checkbook on me. I put them in an envelope and addressed them to myself at General Delivery. You can go down there and find them if you don't believe it."

The officer and the deputy district attorney exchanged glances.

"You mean this *wasn't* a flimflam?" the deputy district attorney asked.

"Of course not. I will admit that I drew a sight draft on H. C. Helmingford. There isn't any such man. I was going to beat it into Los Angeles and take up that sight draft as H. C. Helmingford. But I didn't defraud anyone with that sight draft. I simply put it in for collection."

"What the hell were you trying to do?"

"Build up a banking credit," I said. "I wanted the bank to think I was important. There's no law against that."

"But you gave the automobile company this check, and then drew out all of your balance except two hundred dollars."

"No I didn't. That was on the other bank—or I sure as hell thought it was."

The deputy district attorney rang up the Bank of Commerce. "Has Peter B. Smith got an account there?" he asked.

He held the phone and waited a minute. Then I heard the receiver make noise in his ear. He deliberated for a minute, and said, "I'll call you back in a few minutes."

He said, "Write your name."

I wrote Peter B. Smith.

He said, "Write an order to the post office asking them to deliver to me any mail that's addressed to you and held at General Delivery."

I wrote the order.

"Wait here," the deputy said.

I waited in the office for an hour. When they came back, the man who had sold me the car was with them. "Hello, Smith," he said.

"Hello."

"You caused us a hell of a lot of trouble."

"You caused yourself a hell of a lot of trouble," I said. "My God, you might have known it was all a mistake. Why didn't you get in touch with me? If I'd been a crook, you don't think I'd have left two hundred dollars in the bank, do you? I'd have taken it all."

"Well, what were we supposed to think under the circumstances?"

"How did I know what you were going to think?"

"Look here," he said. "You want that car. It's a good buy. We want the money for it."

"You," I told him, "are going to get slapped in the face with a suit for false arrest and defamation of character."

"Nuts," the deputy district attorney said. "You can't pull that stuff, and you know it. Maybe you made a mistake, but it was *your* mistake, not *theirs.*"

"Go ahead," I said. "Stick up for your taxpayers. I'll import a lawyer. I'll get someone to come in from Los Angeles."

He laughed.

"Well, from Phoenix," I said.

They exchanged glances.

"Look here," the automobile man said. "This has been a mistake all around. It was your mistake. You drew your money out of the wrong bank, or gave us the check on the wrong bank. I don't know which."

"I got mixed up," I admitted.

"All right. You've had an unfortunate experience, and so have we. The governor wouldn't issue extradition papers until we guaranteed to pay all expenses. That cost *us* money. Tell you what we'll do, Smith. You give us the check for sixteen hundred and seventy-two dollars on the Bank of Commerce, and we'll shake hands and forget it. What do you say?"

I said, "I'll give you the check on the Bank of Commerce because I always pay my bills. I'm sorry that mistake was made. But you had no right jumping at hasty conclusions and running to the police. That's going to cost you money."

The deputy district attorney said, "You can't get anywhere with a lawsuit, Smith. As a matter of fact, you're technically guilty. If the automobile people wanted to, they could go ahead and prosecute you."

"Let them prosecute," I said. "Every day I'm in jail is going to cost them a lot of money."

The sheriff entered the conversation. "Look here, boys. This has been a mistake. Now let's get together and do the right thing."

I said, "I wanted the car. I still want the car. I think it's a good car. I'll give him sixteen hundred and seventy-two dollars for it. I made a mistake and drew on the wrong account. That's all."

"And you'll let the rest of it go?" the sheriff asked.

"I didn't say that."

The deputy district attorney said to the automobile man, "Don't do a damn thing until you get a written release from him."

"All right," I surrendered, "draw up the written release, and pass the cigars."

The deputy district attorney typed out the release. I read it carefully. All charges against me were dropped. I agreed not to make any claims against the automobile people, and gave them a complete release of any cause of action I might have against them growing out of the arrest. I said to the deputy district attorney, "I want you and the sheriff to sign it."

"Why?

"Because," I said, "I don't know much about the procedure here, and I don't want to waive my rights and then have something else happen. This just says the automobile people withdraw their charges. How do I know but what you might have a grand jury file against me?"

"Baloney," the deputy district attorney said.

"All right, if it's baloney go ahead and sign. If you don't, I don't."

Everybody signed. I folded the agreement and put it in my pocket. The deputy district attorney gave me a blank check on the Bank of Commerce, and I made it out for the price of the automobile. We all shook hands. The automobile man went back to his office. The deputy sheriff said, "God, it was hot coming across that desert!"

I got up and started pacing the floor, scowling.

The sheriff looked at me and said, "What's the matter, Smith?"

I said, "I've got something on my mind."

There was silence in the room. The two officers and the deputy district attorney were watching me with speculative eyes as I paced the floor.

"What is it?" the sheriff asked. "Maybe we can help you."

"I killed a man," I said.

You could have heard a pin drop.

The deputy district attorney broke the silence. "What was it you did, Smith?" he asked.

"Killed a man," I said, "and my name isn't Smith. It's Lam, Donald Lam."

"Say," the sheriff said, "you're too full of tricks to suit me."

"It isn't a trick," I said. "I came here to take the name of Smith and begin all over again. It wasn't an alias. I just wanted to start life all over, but I guess you can't do that—not when you have a man's soul on your conscience."

"Who did you kill?" the sheriff asked.

"A man by the name of Morgan Birks. You may have read about him. I killed the guy."

I saw glances fly around the table the way a ball team snaps the ball around the infield in between plays. The sheriff said in a kindly tone, "Maybe it would make you feel better if you told us all about it, Lam. How did it happen?"

"I had a job," I said, "as a detective, working for a woman named Bertha Cool. Morgan Birks had a wife. Her name was Sandra, and she had a friend staying with her, Alma Hunter, a girl who's a little bit of all right.

"Well, I was hired to serve papers on Morgan Birks, but I saw someone had been choking Alma Hunter. I asked her about it and she said someone had been in her bedroom. She'd woke up just when he'd clamped down on her throat, and she managed to kick him loose. She was frightened to death.

"She was a good kid, and I started to fall for her. We staged a little necking party in an automobile and I thought she was just what the doctor ordered. I'd have gone to hell for her. Then she told me about this choking business. I didn't want her to stay there in the apartment alone. I put it up to her that I was going to sneak in and spend the night standing guard in the closet. She said I couldn't do that because Sandra Birks slept in the same room. So I told her I was going to come and stay until Sandra got in.

"Well, I went up there, and we talked for a while, and then I saw Sandra was going to be late so I told her to switch out the light and get into bed and I'd wait. I went over and sat down in the closet. I had this gun with me. I tried to keep awake, but I guess I dozed off a bit. I woke up some time in the night and heard Alma Hunter give a little scream. I had a flashlight, and I switched it on. A man was bending over the bed, feeling for her throat. When the flashlight hit him, he turned and started to run. I was pretty much excited. I pulled the trigger, and he went down for the count. I threw the gun on the floor and ran out the door into the corridor. Alma Hunter jumped out of bed and came running after me. The wind slammed the door shut. There was a spring lock on it. She couldn't get back in to get her clothes. She said she'd hide until Sandra came in. We decided there was no use making a squawk to the police. We figured Sandra would help cover the thing up some way. Alma said she'd protect me. So I beat it.

"Then I found that she was trying to take the rap for me, and I figured she could get away with it on account of self-defense, but the last I heard, things didn't look so hot."

The sheriff said, "Sit down, Lam. Sit down, and take it easy. Now don't get all worked up about it. After all, you're going to feel a lot better when you've told us all about it. Now, where did you get the gun?"

"That," I said, "is something else."

"I know it is, Donald, but if you're going to tell the story, you'd better tell the whole story. It isn't going to do any good just to get half of it off your mind. Think of how much better you'll sleep tonight if you come clean and give us the whole thing."

"Bill Cunweather gave me the gun," I said.

"And who's Bill Cunweather?"

"I used to know him back East."

"Where back East?"

"Kansas City."

In the silence that followed, I heard the deputy district attorney take a deep breath.

"Where did you last see Cunweather?" he asked.

"He has a place out on Willoughby Drive."

"Do you remember the number?"

"Nine hundred and seven, I think it is. He's got his whole mob with him."

"Who's in the mob?"

"Oh, everybody," I said. "Fred, and all the rest of them."

"And he gave you the gun?"

"Yes, when I decided to sit up in the room with Alma, I knew that I was going to need some sort of protection. I'm not big enough to protect any girl with my fists. I tried to get Mrs. Cool to give me a gun, and she laughed at me. So I went out to Cunweather. I told him the spot I was in, and he said, 'Hell, Donald, you know where I stand. You can have anything I've got.'"

"Where did Cunweather get the gun?" the deputy district attorney asked.

"His wife was there," I said. "He calls her the little woman. He told her to—say, come to think of it, I guess I hadn't better tell you anything about Cunweather. What difference does it make *where* I got the gun?"

"You knew Cunweather in Kansas City?"

"Sure."

"What did he do there?"

I narrowed my eyes, and said, "I told you we weren't going to talk about Cunweather. I'm talking about me and about Morgan Birks. I guess you know all about it, or you can find out by getting in touch with the people in California."

"We know all about it," the deputy sheriff said. "The newspapers have been full of it. The girl was supposed to have shot him."

I said, "Yes, I know. She was taking the responsibility. I shouldn't have let her do it."

"We're pretty much interested in this gun," the sheriff said.

"Why?"

"When did you get it?"

"The afternoon of the shooting."

"Where?"

"Well, I told Cunweather that I wanted a gun and he said he'd get me one. He asked me where I was going to be later on. I told him I was going to be registered at the Perkins Hotel under the name of Donald Helforth. So he said he'd fix it up to deliver the gun to me there."

"And that's where you got this gun?"

"Yes."

"Who was with you in that hotel, Donald?"

"Alma Hunter. She was registered with me. I think it was room 620."

"And who brought you the gun?"

"A fellow by the name of Jerry Wegley. He was supposed to be a bell captain there in the hotel, but I think he was Cunweather's man. I think Cunweather had planted him on the job."

The sheriff said, "It's going to help a lot if you can prove that, Donald."

"If I can prove what?"

"That about the gun," he said. "The gun was hot. It had been used in a murder in Kansas City."

"In Kansas City?"

"Yes."

"When?"

"A couple of months ago."

"Good God!" I said.

"Can you prove that you got the gun from Jerry Wegley?"

"Why sure. Cunweather won't deny he gave me the gun— well, maybe he will, too, if it was that hot—but maybe Cunweather didn't know."

"He must have known it if it was his gun."

"Well, he had Jerry Wegley get it for me."

"We'd like to take your word for that," the sheriff said.

"You don't have to take my word for it. I can show where I was two months ago. I wasn't anywhere near Kansas City—and I'll tell you something else, when Wegley brought up that gun, he brought up a box of shells for it. I loaded the magazine, and shoved the box with the rest of the shells way in the back part of a bureau drawer in room 620 in the Perkins Hotel. You can search the room and find the shells."

"And you were registered as Donald Helforth there?"

"Yes."

"And you didn't give the gun to Alma Hunter?"

"Hell no! I wanted the gun myself. *She* didn't need a gun. All she had to do was go to sleep. I was going to be on the job to see that nothing happened to her."

The sheriff said, "Well, Donald, you're out of the frying pan and into the fire. I'll have to lock you up now and notify California that I'm holding you."

"I killed him in self-defense," I said.

"He was running away, wasn't he?"

"I guess he was, but you know how those things are. You get pretty excited. I saw him start to run, and it was hard to see just what he *was* doing. I thought perhaps he was reaching for a gun, and—I don't know. I guess I just got excited."

The sheriff said, "Come on, Donald. I'll have to take you back down and put you in the jail. I'll try and make you as comfortable as possible. I'll telephone the officers in California and they'll come and get you."

"Do I have to go back to California again?"

"Sure."

"I don't want to go across that strip of desert while it's hot."

"I don't blame you. They'll probably make it at night."

"How about getting a lawyer?" I asked.

"What good would a lawyer do you?"

"I don't know. I'd like to talk with one."

The sheriff said, "I tell you what, Donald. I think you'd better sign a waiver of extradition and go back to California and face the music. It will look better that way."

I shook my head. "I sign nothing," I said.

"All right, Donald. It's your funeral. I'll have to lock you up. This is a big thing, you know."

CHAPTER TWELVE

THE BED in the jail was hard. The mattress was thin. The night had turned bitterly cold, as so frequently happens in the desert during the early spring. I lay shivering and waiting.

Somewhere a drunk was talking to himself, a thick-tongued soliloquy which ran on and on and on aimlessly, monotonously and unintelligibly. An automobile thief in the next cell was snoring peacefully. I figured it must be midnight. I tried to think of how hot it had been coming across the desert. My thoughts couldn't keep me warm. I thought of Alma—

I heard bolts in the jail door slide back, then I heard the sound of low voices and shuffling feet. Down in the office room, there was the scraping of chair legs along the cement floor. I could hear the scratching of matches and the hum of low-voiced conversation. A door closed and shut out all the noise.

Four or five minutes later, I heard steps coming down the long corridor. The jailer said, "Wake up, Lam. They want you downstairs."

"I want to sleep."

"Well, come on downstairs just the same."

I got up out of bed. It had been too cold to take my

clothes off. The jailer said, "Come on. Don't keep them waiting. Shake a leg."

I followed him down to the office. The district attorney, the sheriff, the deputy district attorney, a shorthand reporter, and two Los Angeles policemen were waiting in the room. A chair had been reserved for me facing a bright light. The sheriff said, "Sit down over in that chair, Donald."

"The light hurts my eyes."

"You'll get accustomed to it after a minute. We want to be where we can see you."

"Well, you don't need to put my eyes out looking at me."

The sheriff said, "If you tell the truth, Donald, we won't have to study your facial expressions to find out when you're lying. If you keep on lying, we're going to have to watch you more closely."

"What makes you think I haven't told the truth?"

He laughed and said, "You've told just enough of the truth, Donald, to convince us that you know what we want to know; but you've stopped a long ways short of telling the truth."

He moved the light a little so that the glare wasn't directly in my eyes.

"Now, Donald," the sheriff said. "These gentlemen are from Los Angeles. They've come all the way across the desert to hear your story. They know enough to know that you've been lying, but some of what you said is true. Now we want the rest of it."

He talked with the fatherly tone one uses in dealing with a half idiot. Cops usually use that approach in talking with crooks—and the crooks usually fall for it.

I pretended to fall for it, too.

"That's all I know," I said sullenly. "What I told you today."

The light switched up so that the glare struck me full in my aching eyes. The sheriff said, "I'm afraid, Donald, I'm going to have to go over this with you bit by bit, and watch your facial expressions."

"To hell with that stuff!" I said. "That's the old hooey. You're giving me the third degree."

"No, we're not giving you any third degree, Donald—that is, I'm not. But this is a serious matter, and we want to get the truth."

"What's wrong with my story?" I asked.

"Everything," he said. "In the first place, you weren't there in that room, Donald. Some of the things you said about Cunweather are true but not all of them. You didn't shoot Morgan. The girl shot Morgan. You gave her the gun. She dropped the gun and ran out. She called you from the telephone booth downstairs. A tenant in the building gave her a nickel with which to put through the call. Your landlady had to get you up out of bed— Now then, Donald, we want the *truth*."

I said, "Oh, all right. Turn that damn light out of my eyes and I'll tell you everything."

The district attorney cleared his throat. "Take this," he said to the shorthand reporter. "Now, Donald, as I understand it, you're going to make a voluntary statement or confession. This is the result of your own volition. No promises or inducements have been made to you; nor have any threats been made. You're going to make a statement simply because you want to tell the truth and make a clean breast of the entire situation. Is that right?"

"Have it your own way," I said.

"That doesn't answer my question, Donald."

"Oh, hell," I said, "you've got me. What's the use?"

He turned to the shorthand reporter. "The answer is yes," he said. "Take it down. That's right, isn't it, Donald?"

"Yes."

"Go ahead," the sheriff said. "Let's hear the truth, Donald. But remember, we don't want any more lying."

He deflected the light so that my tortured eyeballs had a rest. "Go ahead, Donald."

"I killed him," I said, "but Alma Hunter doesn't know it. And I didn't do it because I was guarding Alma Hunter. I did it because I was told to."

"Who told you to?"

"Bill Cunweather."

The sheriff said, "Now, Donald, we don't want any more lies."

"You're getting the real low-down now."

"All right. Go ahead."

'Do you want it from the beginning?" I asked.

"Yes, from the beginning."

"Well," I said, "I used to know the Cunweather outfit in Kansas City. I'm not going to tell you a thing about who I really am because my father and mother are living, and I'm not going to break their hearts. But you can take it from me that I've batted around. But I didn't have nothing to do with that Kansas City job. I was in California when that job was pulled, and I can prove it.

"Well, here's the low-down. Cunweather was the head of the slot-machine racket. Naturally, there was a pay-off. I don't know all the dope on that, but it ran into quite a wad of dough. Morgan Birks was the pay-off man.

"Well, things ran along pretty smooth until the grand jury started investigating. A citizens' vice committee had some undercover men out and they uncovered the whole racket. They knew the names of some of the guys who were getting the dough. They didn't know the higher-ups, but they knew some of the contact men and they knew how much those men were getting.

"Well, that was where things began to get interesting, because there was a leak from the grand jury; and we found that the undercover men for the citizens' committee reported that the pay-off was just about half of what Cunweather thought it was. In other words, every time Morgan Birks would collect ten thousand dollars to pay off to the big shots, he'd salt five grand and pass on only half of what he'd collected as the real pay-off.

"Los Angeles is a tough city to do business in, and Morgan Birks had specified that if anything was going to be done, he had to have the exclusive handling of the whole business. Morgan Birks had been with Cunweather for some time, and the chief—that's Cunweather—figured he was absolutely on the up-and-up.

"Well, when this blow-off came, Morgan Birks took it on the lam, the idea being that he was hiding out from the grand jury. He wasn't. He was hiding out from the chief because he was afraid the chief was going to rub him out.

"Morgan Birks had been pretty smart. He'd cached most of the swag in safety deposit boxes, and these safety deposit boxes were in his wife's name. Well, it happened that that was the particular time his wife chose to start a divorce action, knowing that she had him over a barrel. She'd been laying for a break like that because she'd been stepping and Morgan had the goods on her.

"That raised merry hell with Morgan Birks. He couldn't go into court to fight the divorce action. She had all of the stuff where she could get at it and he couldn't. He had to take things lying down. So he reached an agreement with her—the best he could get—which wasn't much. He had the deadwood on her, but he couldn't use it because of what she had on him and because the chief would have taken him for a ride if he'd stuck his head out of cover."

"Where was Morgan Birks?" the district attorney asked.

"I'm coming to that," I said. "You said you wanted it from the beginning."

"All right. Go ahead and give it to me."

"Well, the chief found out that Sandra Birks was going to hire the Cool Detective Agency to serve the papers. So the chief planted me to get a job with the Cool Detective Agency, figuring that we'd find Morgan that way. I got the job and was assigned to serve the papers. Sandra Birks naturally wanted the thing cleaned up.

"Now, Sandra was protecting Morgan Birks, but we didn't know it at the time. She had a man in the house who was supposed to be her brother. It wasn't her brother at all. It was Morgan. But Morgan was watching her like a hawk. He was afraid she was going to two-time him all the way along the line and skip out with all the money from the safety deposit boxes instead of the cut that they'd agreed on.

"Well, as soon as I'd get any information from Sandra Birks and Alma Hunter I'd relay it on to the chief. And in that way, we found out where Morgan Birks was hiding—that is, we found out the man who was supposed to be Sandra's brother was really the man we wanted."

"But how could he pose as her brother when you already knew him?" the sheriff asked.

"Because he'd pretended he was in an automobile accident, and they'd taped a lot of stuff over his nose, and the tape had pulled his face all out of shape. He was combing his hair differently, and he'd put on some padding under his coat, enough to fill him out. After I bumped Morgan off, I rolled that padding up into a bundle and dropped it in an ashcan in front of the apartment house. You can check on that."

"Go ahead," the sheriff said.

"Well, I passed all this information on to the chief. So the chief had a pug by the name of Fred—I never did know his last name. And he sent Fred out to bring Morgan Birks to time.

"Well, here's the funny thing. Sandra had already been down and looted the lock boxes. She was lousy with coin. Morgan Birks found it out, and made up his mind he'd kill her, get the dough, and skip out. But Sandra was playing around with a boy friend, and she didn't want Morgan to know anything about it. So she talked Alma Hunter into sleeping in her bed. She told her husband she was going to be sleeping in one of the twin beds in the room with Alma—and he wasn't to come in because he was supposed to be her brother.

"Her husband had his keys. Along in the middle of the night he slipped into the apartment, tiptoed over to the twin bed, groped around in the dark, and started to choke Alma Hunter, thinking it was Sandra. Alma kicked him in the stomach a couple of times and broke loose his hold. She started to scream, and Morgan beat it. That was the day before I bumped Morgan off.

"Well, when the chief got the dope on Morgan, naturally Morgan was on the spot. Morgan confessed to everything and agreed to return the dough. But he couldn't return the dough until he got it back from his wife. So the chief told him to go get it.

"But get this—the chief wasn't trusting Morgan Birks any more, and Morgan knew too much. With the grand jury business coming up and Sandra Birks turning against him and all of that stuff, Morgan represented a pretty bad liability.

"Now, I'd taken a shine to Alma Hunter. She was a good kid, and when I found out that Morgan had been at work on her throat, I slipped her the rod and told her to protect herself in case anything else happened.

"Well, Morgan met me at a drug store where the chief had staked me out, and we were going up to get the dough from Sandra. Morgan told me Alma Hunter was out with a boy friend and wouldn't be in all evening. Do you get the sketch? Sandra Birks had the chief's dough. We wanted it. We knew it was going to be a rough party. Sandra had passed a stall on to Morgan. He'd fallen for it, and passed it on to me. Morgan figured I'd tap her over the head and get the dough she was supposed to be wearing in a money belt under her nightgown right next to the skin.

"I fell for it. We went up to the apartment. Morgan Birks opened it with his key, and went into the bedroom. It was dark. I had a flashlight, but Morgan said his wife always woke up when there was a light in the room and for me to feel my way. I'd asked him just before we went in if there was anyone except his wife in the place, and he said no, his wife was the only one there.

"I fumbled my way along through the dark. I could hear her breathing there on the bed. I decided I'd clap my hand over her mouth and then grab the money belt. Morgan Birks was over near the foot of the bed somewhere. I couldn't see just where, but I could hear him breathing, too. I reached out, trying to get my hand where I could clamp it over her mouth all at once. I wanted to get it where I could feel from her breathing that it was right over her nose. I stuck it out there in the dark and kept moving it around until I could feel her breath on the palm of my hand—well, then she woke up.

"And I swear to heaven, gentlemen, that I never had a chance. She was quicker than a cat. That rod came around and blazed off in my face before I could do a thing about it. I'd made a grab for her, but she'd moved and all I got was a handful of pillow. And then this gun went off right under my nose, and then she jumped out of bed and made for the door. And as soon as I heard that scream, I knew it was Alma and not Sandra.

"Well, we stood there for a minute until we heard the outer door slam, and then I turned on my flash. Morgan Birks said, 'You dirty bungler. You've ranked the job!'

"I didn't say anything. I was looking at the rod on the floor. I knew it was the gun I'd given Alma Hunter. She'd shot and then dropped it when she'd beat it for the door. Morgan Birks was still cussing me. I reached down and picked up the gun. I said, 'Birks, you can't shoot square even when it's a showdown, can you?' He said, 'What do you mean?' I said, 'You know damn well what I mean. You planted Alma Hunter on me and said it was Sandra.'

"I think he read what was going to happen then in my eyes. He ran past me and tried to get to the door. Well, he never made it. I shot him through the back of the head. Then I dropped the gun on the floor and had to move the body back in order to open the door. I went out to the corridor, down the back stairs, out through the alley door, took a taxicab, went home, and went to bed."

"Did you report to Cunweather?"

"Not then. I figured that was the way the chief would like to have things and there was no use getting all excited about it."

"Did you go to sleep?"

"I was just getting to sleep when Alma Hunter called me on the telephone. I hadn't expected she'd do that— Well, you know the rest. I put on an act about being sleepy so that the landlady had to call me three or four times."

The sheriff said, "By God, I believe you, Lam."

The district attorney said, "Wait a minute. That would mean the gun was fired twice."

"Sure, it was fired twice," I said.

"What became of the first bullet?"

"How the hell do I know? It's stuck in something."

"The gun couldn't have been fired twice," one of the Los Angeles officers said. "The magazine holds seven shells. There were six shells in the gun when the boys from Homicide found it."

I said, "I'm telling the truth. I can prove it. I loaded that gun myself. I put seven shells in the magazine, then I jacked one up into the barrel. Then I took the magazine out again, and put an extra shell in. That made eight shells. You get the box of shells in the bureau drawer of room 620 in the Perkins Hotel, and you'll find there are eight shells gone from the box."

The sheriff said, "He's right. That accounts for that extra empty cartridge they found in the room."

The two men from California got up. "Well, Donald," one of them said, "you're going back with us. Get your things, and we'll start now."

"I don't want to start now," I said. "And I don't have to."

"What do you mean?"

"I'm in Arizona," I told him. "I don't like California. It's too damn hot going across the desert. I'm getting along fine here. I like the jail, and I like the treatment. You give me the dose here and I'll take it."

"Surely, Donald, you aren't going to make us go to the bother of getting extradition, are you?"

"I'm not going to leave here."

One of the cops moved forward belligerently. "Why, you dirty—" The sheriff put a hand on his arm. "Not here, buddy," he said in a slow drawl that packed plenty of authority.

The district attorney said to the jailor, "Take him back to his cell. We've got some telephoning to do."

"I want a paper and a pen," I said.

They exchanged glances, then the sheriff nodded. "The jailor will bring them to you."

I went back to my cell. It was so cold I could hardly keep my knees from knocking together, but I sat there with chattering teeth and wrote by the dim light of a jail incandescent.

After an hour they came back for me. The sheriff said, "The stenographer has written out the confession you made. We want to read it to you, and if it's correct, we want you to sign it."

"Sure," I said, "I'll sign it, but here's something that I want filed."

"What is it?" he asked, looking at the scrawled pages.

"That," I said, "is the application of Donald Lam, also known as Peter B. Smith, for a writ of *habeas corpus*."

The sheriff said, "Donald, you must be crazy. You've confessed to cold-blooded, deliberate, premeditated murder."

"Sure," I said. "I killed a rat. Are you going to file this application for *habeas corpus*, or do I refuse to sign the confession?"

"I'll file it," he said. "I thought you were just a stircrazy punk. Now I know you're nuts."

CHAPTER THIRTEEN

THE COURTROOM was packed with sweltering humanity. Outside, the sun was melting the pavement in the streets. It was ten o'clock in the morning, but it was already hot. Out in the open air, the heat was dry and easy to bear. Inside the crowded courtroom, the air was soaked with the perspiration of curious spectators.

Judge Raymond C. Oliphant came in and took his seat on the bench. The bailiff called the court to order. The judge looked down at me with curious but kindly eyes. "This is the time heretofore fixed," he said, "for hearing the application of Donald Lam, also known as Peter B. Smith, for the writ of *habeas corpus*. Are you ready, Mr. Lam?"

"Yes, your honor."

"Have you a lawyer to represent you?"

"No."

"Do you intend to secure one?"

"No."

"I believe you have some funds, Mr. Lam?"

"Yes, I have."

"You're able to hire an attorney if you want one?"

"I am."

"And you don't want one?"

"No, your honor."

The judge turned to the district attorney.

"Ready for the state," the district attorney said.

"You have filed a return to the writ?" the judge asked.

"We have, your honor. It sets forth that the defendant is being held in custody by virtue of a warrant for his arrest for first-degree murder issued in the State of California. Extradition proceedings are being taken, and we expect at any moment to have the requisition flown to Phoenix by plane, and have a writ of extradition issued by the governor of Arizona. I believe I am safe in assuming that this will be done within a matter of hours."

"And that is the only reason that the defendant is being held?" Judge Oliphant asked.

"Yes, your honor."

"There is no doubt as to the identity of the defendant?"

"No, your honor."

"Very well, put on your evidence."

The district attorney called the sheriff. The sheriff related the circumstances of my arrest. He called the court stenographer, and the stenographer read my statement into evidence.

Judge Oliphant looked down at me rather kindly. "I think," he said, "that this is enough proof. You seem, Mr. Lam, to have confessed to what may or may not be first-degree murder. At any rate, it is homicide. The question of degree, the malice, and the amount of premeditation will have to be determined by the California courts. But it is apparent to this court that you are guilty of either first- or second-degree murder. It is, therefore—"

Thanks to the activities of the grievance committee, most of my legal experience had consisted of following involved legal doctrines through the intricacies of a law library. My courtroom experience had been very limited, and my knees were rather wobbly as I got to my feet. But I was mad enough to keep my voice from quavering as I interrupted him.

"Is it the custom, your honor, to decide a case before the petitioner has had an opportunity to make any showing?" I asked.

He frowned, and said, "I was trying to be easy on you. Go ahead and put on your case if you want to. You'll just give the California authorities more— I think you should have a lawyer, Mr. Lam."

"I don't want any lawyer," I said, and called the officer who had taken me to Yuma as my first witness.

"What's your name?" I asked.

"Claude Flinton."

"You are an officer of this state?"

"Yes."

"And you brought me to Yuma?"

"That's right."

"From where?"

"From El Centro."

"Did I leave El Centro voluntarily?"

He laughed and said, "You did not. The sheriff of El Centro and I dragged you out and put you in a car, and it was a hot job."

"Under what authority?"

"Because I had a writ of extradition and a warrant of arrest on a felony embezzlement charge with a count of obtaining property under false pretenses."

"What did you do with me?"

"Took you back to Arizona and lodged you here in jail in Yuma."

"Did I accompany you of my own free will?"

He grinned and said, "You did not."

I said, "That's all."

The judge asked in icy tones, "Have you any more witnesses, Mr. Lam?"

"None, your honor."

"Very well. I shall now decide the case."

"Will I have an opportunity to argue it?"

"I fail to see where you can say anything which will affect the ruling of the court."

I said, "There is plenty to be said, your honor. The State of California wants me back. A few hours ago, the State of California didn't want me within its borders. The State of California turned me over to the State of Arizona against my will and wish. I was dragged into the State of Arizona. There can be no question of that."

"But what does that have to do with it?" the judge asked. "You have admitted killing a man in California."

"Certainly, I killed him. He deserved to die. He was a rat and a double-crosser. But that isn't the question before this court. The question before this court is whether I can be extradited to California. I can't be extradited to California. The only authority which one state has to take prisoners from another state comes from the organic law which provides that fugitives from justice may be extradited from one sovereign state to another. I am not a fugitive from justice."

"If you're not a fugitive from justice, I don't know what you are," Judge Oliphant said.

"I don't need to argue the matter," I retorted, "for two reasons. One of them is that your honor's mind is evidently made up, and the other is that better legal minds than I have already wrestled with the problem. The fact remains, however, that a man is not a fugitive from a state unless he flees from that state. He doesn't flee from that state unless he does so voluntarily and in order to avoid arrest. I did not flee from California. I was dragged from California. I was taken out under legal process to answer for a crime of which I was innocent. I claimed that I was innocent. I came to Arizona and established my innocence. Any time I get good and ready to go back to California, California can arrest me for murder. Until I get good and ready to go back, I can stay here and no power on earth can make me budge."

The judge was looking interested now. "When you mention that more learned minds than yours have considered the question, are you, by any chance, referring to some judicial precedent?"

"I am, your honor. The case of *In re Whittington,* 34C.A.344, is a leading case and absolutely in point. I can also refer you to the case of *People* vs. *Jones,* S4C.A.423. The California doctrine has been succinctly expressed in Volume 12 California Jurisprudence, page 398, as follows: 'Where it appears that the presence of the accused in the state of refuge is not due to any voluntary act of his own, but to legal or illegal compulsion, he is not a fugitive from justice and cannot be extradited as such. Thus where it is shown that his presence in the state of refuge is due to extradition proceedings instituted by that state itself for a previous crime and honored by the state now demanding his return, he cannot be extradited by the latter, both because he did not flee from it, and because, by honoring the first requisition, it waived any right to prosecute him for the offense committed against its laws.'"

The judge sat staring at me incredulously. The district attorney got to his feet, and said, "Surely, your honor, that cannot be the law. If such were the law, any man could commit murder,

with malice aforethought. He could coldly, deliberately, and fe-
loniously kill another human being; then, by taking advantage
of a legal loophole, avoid any punishment."

Judge Oliphant said slowly, "And apparently that is exactly what the petitioner in this case has done. It needs no great
imagination to realize that, step by step, he has embarked
upon a course of carefully planned murder with diabolical ingenuity. If this is the law, this man has committed the perfect
crime, not as it is usually planned, with such subtlety that the
clues are completely concealed, but with such ingenuity that
he cannot be punished. It is to be noted that the petitioner
has memorized the text of that portion of California Jurisprudence dealing with the point he is making. It is, therefore, readily apparent that the full possibilities of the situation have been carefully thought out by him well in advance.
The entire history of this case indicates that the petitioner is
possessed of an astute legal mind which, unfortunately, is not
balanced by a corresponding sense of legal ethics. However
much the Court may deplore the latter, it cannot ignore the
consummate brilliance with which this petitioner, frail in his
physical appearance, apparently young, innocent and inexpe-
rienced, has jockeyed the authorities of two states into such a
position that they are apparently powerless to punish him for
a cold-blooded, premeditated, and deliberate murder, his part
in which he has brazenly admitted. It is an astounding situation. To some extent, the defendant's moral and legal lapse
is atoned by his confession which has enabled the California
authorities to arrest the petitioner's accomplices. However, the
fact remains that the petitioner at bar, despite his very apparent youth and inexperience, has the ability to discover, and
the ingenuity to carry into execution, a scheme by which he

has adroitly outwitted the sovereign authorities of two states. It is a most astounding situation.

"The court will take a thirty-minute recess during which the court will endeavor to consider this matter with a fair and impartial mind. However, the court cannot remain unaware of the seriousness of leaving such a legal loophole in our social and legislative structure. The court will not construe the organic law cited by the petitioner in the light of the petitioner's contention unless it appears that the State of California has estopped itself from asking for a different construction by a decision which is plain and unequivocal in its language."

Judge Oliphant got up and walked gravely into chambers. I sat there waiting in the courtroom. After a few moments, the sheriff said, "This way, Donald."

He took me into his office. I sat there waiting. The district attorney came in and looked at me as though I was something other than human.

At the end of half an hour, the sheriff took me back into court. Judge Oliphant came in and took his seat on the bench. His shoulders were sagging. He looked down at the district attorney, and said, "The court has no other alternative. The law in this case is exactly as contended by the petitioner. Under this law a man could—and has—committed a cold-blooded murder with complete legal immunity. Posing as a not-too-bright young criminal, he has victimized the law itself. There can be no question in the mind of the court but what the shrewd and unscrupulous intelligence of the petitioner in this case has carefully planned each step in a well-laid campaign. However, there is no legal proof before the court indicating that such is the case. The California decisions cited by the petitioner are absolutely in point. In view of the interpretation which has been placed upon the law by the courts of California, it would be idle to contend for any other interpretation. California has passed upon the matter, and the California courts have precluded themselves from seeking any other interpretation of the law. California cannot extradite this man. The petitioner is discharged from custody, much as the court regrets the necessity of making such a decision."

The district attorney said, "Your honor, we don't need to believe his story. We can hold him for further developments. Perhaps he—"

"Apparently you don't appreciate the diabolical ingenuity of the petitioner's position," Judge Oliphant said. "He can't be extradited from Arizona. He isn't a fugitive from justice—not from California at any rate. I doubt if there is enough evidence to connect him with this Kansas City crime. If there is, there will be little difficulty in finding the petitioner. He certainly is not going to leave the State of Arizona. Here he enjoys legal immunity. Elsewhere, he would not, and the perspicacity of this petitioner is such that he not only realizes that fact but will take full technical advantage of it. I even doubt if he could be extradited to Kansas City. The petitioner is discharged."

A slow murmur grew in volume from the crowd in the courtroom. It was not a hostile murmur. It was a murmur of surprise and of interest. Had an attorney been representing me, I probably would have been lynched. As it was, I had been the underdog, standing alone and unaided at the bar of justice. I had forced the judge to accept my interpretation of the law and had whipped the astounded district attorney to a standstill.

Someone applauded.

Someone laughed.

The judge ordered the courtroom cleared, and then adjourned court.

CHAPTER FOURTEEN

THE CLERK at the Phoenix Hotel said, "Mrs. Cool arrived by airplane from California. She had rather a rough trip and was quite upset. She left word that under no circumstances was she to be disturbed."

I showed him the telegram she'd sent. "I'm the one she came to see," I said. "Here's her telegram telling me to meet her here at the earliest possible moment."

The clerk hesitated a moment, then nodded to the telephone operator. "You may ring," he said.

A moment later, the operator said, "You may go up, Mr. Lam. Room 319."

I took the elevator to the third floor, knocked on the door of 319, and Bertha Cool said, "Come in. God damn it, don't stand out there making a racket."

I turned the knob and opened the door. She was propped up in bed. A wet towel was wrapped around her forehead. There was no make-up on her face. The muscles sagged down, pulling her lips down at the corners, emphasizing her battleship jaw.

"Donald," she asked, "did you ever ride in an airplane?"

I nodded.

"Did you get seasick?"

"No."

"I did," she said. "My God I thought that damn plane would never get here. Donald, my love, what the hell have you been doing?"

"Various things," I said.

"I'll say you have! You've been giving the agency a lot of publicity."

I found myself a chair and dropped into it.

"No, not there, Donald. It hurts to turn my head. Come over here and sit on the foot of the bed—there, that's better. Donald, are you in love with that girl?"

"Yes."

"Did you do this because you loved her?"

"Partially," I said, "and partially because I couldn't resist the temptation to blow up some of the smug legal theories entertained by a lot of mossback lawyers. The grievance committee said my idea a bombproof murder could be committed was an indication I didn't have a very good foundation in my legal education. They didn't bother to find out what the scheme was, but, just because they *thought* a man couldn't commit a murder and beat the rap legally, they figured I was wrong in saying he could. I wanted to show 'em. If they hadn't suspended me from the bar, I'd have made a name for myself before this."

"Do you know any more tricks like that?" she asked.

"Lots of them," I said.

"Donald, my lamb, light a cigarette and put it between my lips." I lit the cigarette, put it in between the heavy lips. She sucked in a deep drag, and said, "You and I can go a long way together. You've got brains—you little runt. But you've got to get over being so impulsive and so damn chivalrous. My God, Donald, at your age you're going to fall in love and bounce back out again a dozen times before you settle down to one woman. You mark my words, Donald. I know. But you have a fine mind, Donald, my love. You're a jewel—how the hell did you know what had happened, Donald?"

I said, "It was a cinch when I got to thinking it over. Someone heard a shot and notified the police. The police didn't come until quite a while after Alma Hunter had left the apartment. I figured the person who notified the police must have heard a second shot, and no one had heard the first shot. The magazine held seven shells. There were only six in the gun. Alma's bullet hit someone. Morgan Birks must have been shot, just as the police claim, while he was trying to get out of the door. Death was instantaneous. Therefore, he must have fallen in such a position that it was impossible to get the door open without moving his body. Alma Hunter didn't move any body. She opened the door and ran out. Cunweather was interested in finding Morgan Birks. Cunweather had an organization. The slot-machine racket wasn't a one-man business. It called for an organization. Morgan Birks was really hiding from his own organization. Sandra Birks had a lot of money in safety deposit boxes. Both Morgan and Sandra were trying to keep anyone from knowing about it. Sandra was trying to get it from Morgan. Alma slept in Sandra's bed, and someone tried to choke her, someone with long fingernails. I noticed that Bleatie had slender, tapering hands, something like a woman. The fingers were long, and the nails were well manicured. If Sandra had died there wouldn't have been any divorce. Morgan had Cunweather fooled on the Bleatie business, but Cunweather didn't stay fooled. When he was beating up on me he'd have given a lot to have found Morgan Birks. When you went out and tried to shake him down, he didn't give a damn. That meant he'd doped out what had happened after he realized I'd served the papers there in the hotel. It meant he'd already put the screws on Morgan Birks. Which one of the Cunweather gang was wounded?"

"Fred," she said. "Alma's shot hit him in the upper left arm. My God, Donald, do you know everything?"

"No," I said. "But I told you when you hired me, I was never very strong as a boy. I couldn't fight, so I had to think. I developed an imagination and an ability to scheme."

She said, "You could have gone about solving this case without dragging yourself into it. My God, Donald, think of the chances you took—and think of the advertising I got! It's tremendous, you darling!"

I said, "How could I have gone about it any other way? The gun was tied up to me, and the gun was hot. If I'd tried to tell the police what really happened, they'd have laughed at me. I could have advanced a theory—and the police would never have paid any attention to it—not after Alma Hunter told her story."

"How did you spot Cunweather?"

"That was easy. Cunweather had a tip-off there was going to be action in the Perkins Hotel. He had a man planted there. That man knew everything I did. The bell captain knew everything I did. Therefore, the bell captain must have been Cunweather's man. They played me for a sucker. They slipped me a hot gun, and then Cunweather had Fred work me over. I told them I was going to get even with them. By God, I did. I could have accused them until I was black in the face, and never got anywhere. It took a confession to get action."

She grinned, and said, "Yes, Donald, my love, you got action. If you'd been in California and seen that action you'd have been satisfied. After you confessed they certainly went to work on Cunweather. I heard they worked him over with a rubber hose. He wilted like a hot lettuce leaf. If he beats the rap on the Morgan Birks murder they're going after him on the Kansas City kill. It's a damn nice case. Donald, run down and get me a flask of whisky."

"I'll need some expense money," I said.

"What did you do with all the cash Sandra Birks gave you?"

"I salted it away."

"How much was it?"

"I can't tell you offhand," I said.

"About how much, Donald?"

"I can't tell you."

"Was it ten grand?"

"I'm sure I can't say."

"Where do you have it hidden, Donald, darling?"

"In a safe place."

Her eyes narrowed. "Remember, Donald, my lamb, that you're working for *me.*"

I said, "Yes. So far as finances are concerned, I believe I'm indebted to you, am I not—for taxicab fare?"

"That's right," she said without batting an eyelash. "Ninety-five cents. It comes out of your first pay check. Don't worry about it, Donald, because I'm not. It's all duly entered as a debit on your salary account."

"By the way," I asked, "who was Dr. Holoman? Was he really Sandra's sweetie?"

"Yes. They had Morgan Birks lashed to the mast. As Sandra's brother, Morgan had to sit by and watch her flirt with this chap who was masquerading as Dr. Holoman. If he'd asserted his rights as a husband, Cunweather would have rubbed him out, after squeezing the last dime of the hold-out money out of him."

"Sandra," I said, "seems to be an opportunist."

"She is. How about that whisky, Donald?"

"How about the money?"

She reached for her purse.

"You flew down alone?" I asked as she fumbled through some loose bills.

"Not me," she said. "When Bertha Cool travels she has someone with her to pay expenses—unless there's been a damn fat retainer paid. No, Donald, I brought my client along. She's in the next room. She doesn't know you're here yet. She's been talking about you a lot—all the way down. My God, there I was, sick as a horse, and she was talking about you."

"You mean Sandra?" I asked.

"Hell, no," she said, jerking her head toward the door to the communicating room. "Sandra will fall for you when you're there, but she forgets you when you're away."

I walked across and opened the door. Alma Hunter was sitting in a chair near the window. When she saw me, she got to her feet and stood staring at me with starry eyes and crimson half-parted lips.

"Here's the money for the whisky, Donald," Mrs. Cool called. "Don't get mushy, my pet. God knows you haven't a God damn cent to get married on, and you owe me ninety-five cents for taxi fare."

I walked on into Alma's room and kicked the communicating door shut with my heel.

THE END

DISCUSSION QUESTIONS

- Were you able to predict any part of the solution to the case?

- Aside from the solution, did anything about the book surprise you? If so, what?

- Did any aspects of the plot date the story? If so, which ones?

- Would the story be different if it were set in the present day? If so, how?

- What role did the setting play in the narrative?

- For those familiar with Erle Stanley Gardner's Perry Mason novels, how did this compare?

- Can you think of any contemporary mystery authors that seem to be influenced or inspired by Erle Stanley Gardner's writing?

ERLE STANLEY GARDNER

from

AMERICAN MYSTERY CLASSICS

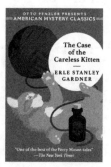

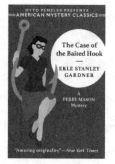